JANET K. SHAWGO

The Bishop's Palace

First edition

ISBN: 978-1-73-340453-2

Editing by Joan Acklin
Cover art by Michelle Rene
Proofreading by Leanne Yarrow & Diane Garland

This book was professionally typeset on Reedsy.
Find out more at reedsy.com

To friends and family who shine their light, when we find ourselves in dark places.

Contents

Chapter 1

The Bishop's Palace
  Summer 1890

The Spanish moss failing to sway in the trees and the absence of sounds in the Louisiana night could be considered ill omens. Even heaven refused to cooperate with a moonless night, making the task ahead of him a difficult one. The figure of a man moved through the dead with a small lantern, crossing himself and asking the virgin mother for protection.

The sound of boys arguing stopped his journey allowing him to breathe easier, knowing they were still alive. He moved silently through the black front gate of the graveyard, asking himself the same question each time he came out to this place. Why are bravery and stupidity always wasted on the young? It appeared these three boys were perfect examples of both. He waited a moment, listening to their conversation before moving toward them.

"You ain't got any guts if you don't go in there, Jacque," the older boy chided the smallest of the three.

"Don't need guts, Andre. I want to live, ain't no one ever come out that goes in there," Jacque told him.

"Baby stories ya mama is telling to scare you," Rey added.

"No such things as demons, and you need to learn it now," Andre said.

"My mama don't tell stories. I'll fight you for saying so," Jacque responded, stepping toward Rey.

"You boys have no business here."

The three hadn't heard the figure close in on them, jumping when addressed.

Andre dropped his head, staring at the ground. "Mr. Leotis, we weren't doing no harm, trying to make a man outta Jacque."

"If you intend to become men, this is not the place for you," he told all of them.

The three kicked the dirt with their bare feet.

"I never thought a strong man like you would believe such stuff," Rey said.

Leotis walked through them, looking at the building of stone and iron untouched by time. The first glow of light inside made him turn back toward them. "The Bishop's Palace is a place of evil, and if you enter, the holy mother cannot protect you from the demon inside. I'll not let your mothers cry over empty coffins. Go home and never return."

Before anyone could speak, the scream of a man startled all of them. They turned to see a glow coming from several windows. Leotis took a stance in front of the boys holding up the lantern.

"I think you're right Mr. Leotis. We should go home," Andre said.

"Be respectful as you go through the cemetery and say a prayer of forgiveness, understood?"

"Yes, sir," they all said.

"Now get." He watched as the three hurried toward the black gate, stopping to make the sign of the cross before entering. Leotis took one last look at the Bishop's Palace, slowly backing away. The boys were waiting on the other side of the cemetery for him.

"Mr. Leotis, what makes you so sure there is evil inside and not drifters looking for a place to sleep?" Rey asked.

He motioned for them to move away so their conversation would not disturb the dead. "My older brother and his friends thought as you. When the time arrived to prove their worth as men, the Bishop's Palace called, pulling strongly at them. Two dismissed their faith, daring the devil one night."

"What happened?" Jacque asked.

"My brother came home no longer able to speak."

"What about his friends?" Andre asked.

Leotis shook his head. "I'll speak no more of my brother or the bishop, and neither should you."

The boys moved closer to Leotis as they walked away from the dead, repeating the rosary with every step taken.

Chapter 2

August 25th, 1890
San Francisco, California

Morlanna Miller gripped the leather case and her purse tightly as the streetcar headed up Market Street. The sounds of horses and motor vehicles filled the town with flowing life as only the city of San Francisco could provide. The smell of fresh bread and pastries made her wish the last block of the journey had been on foot. She missed breakfast this morning, and the scent of cinnamon and sugar made her stomach rumble with hunger. It was an important day, as all the research over the past six months would define her success or failure as a reporter.

Her employer, the *Worth Daily News*, was a well-respected newspaper in the city. She knew it would be difficult to convince the owner this particular story contained substance. The disappearance of a Catholic Bishop over seventy years ago wasn't a significant story until you added the possibility of a pirate's treasure. The additional information of men and boys entering a crumbling building searching for wealth and never returning left families mourning. She could not prove the existence of treasure, but the people in the parish swore it to be true. This information of legend and myth should be enough to garner the interest of a curious public. Sarah Winchester's passion for mystics and seances increased after the death of her husband and daughter. She believed their deaths were payback due to those killed by the Winchester weapons and began building a home directed by the spirits. Stories such as this and a legendary bishop would fuel enthusiasm for her story.

The shaky elevator ride to the fourth floor of the newspaper always alarmed her. The alternative would be taking the stairs, but that could cause perspiration stains indicating she might be nervous or unprepared. The work floor looked busy as she entered, forcing a quick check of the watch pendant showing the time to be seven-thirty. She walked to her desk, removed the over jacket and hat, placing them on a coat stand.

"Miss Miller!"

She turned to face the owner of the newspaper. "Yes, sir."

He opened his pocket watch and then looked at her. "My office and bring your research," he demanded.

She raised her eyebrow and took a deep breath. "Good morning to you, too." She removed the file from the leather case hesitating for a moment.

"Steady, Morlanna, keep your temper today," she whispered.

There was always an uneasy feeling when she entered Mr. Ludsworth's office. The rumors of his unsavory sexual appetite were nauseating. The stories of his escapades were legendary and spoken in the office corners. A proper woman should not listen to such gossip, but necessary to protect her reputation from any improprieties. She stood in the doorway of his office and waited. A chill ran over her as he raised his head, gazing up and down her figure.

Milford Ludsworth stood approximately five-foot-six, in his mid-fifties, heavyset, with a full head of brown hair and disgusting unkept bushy mustache. As the owner of the newspaper, his enormous wealth made him a well-respected citizen of San Francisco. His frequent visits to the opium dens and brothels in the city were overlooked by society and his wife.

He held out a hand. "Do you have something for me to read?"

"I do."

His face turned red. "Then give it to me and shut the door."

"My pleasure, sir." She walked forward and placed the file on his desk instead of handing it to him.

He glared at her in frustration. "Sit down."

She took two steps back, settling in the hard straight-back chair. The crinkle of the long brown skirt and creaking of the wooden floor echoed in the large office. Several times over the next thirty minutes, he would stop reading and look at her. He leaned back in his chair, lighting a cigar as he completed her report. A moment later he blew smoke across the desk into Morlanna's face. She never blinked nor moved a hand to whisk away the stench, as it would indicate weakness. Months of her research lay in the hands of a man who could allow the story to move forward or end up in the trash bin.

"Miss Miller, you do, realize this is a legitimate newspaper and not some spiritual rag for the simple-minded," he said.

She cleared her throat. "Milford, I hardly believe Mrs. Winchester would agree with your opinion on her beliefs."

His face turned red as he pushed away from the desk, standing up and pointing at her. "Everyone in the building is aware I despise being called by my given name. Are you trying my patience, or do you wish to be fired from your job? As for that foolish woman spending her late husband's fortune on that atrocity, at the instruction of spirits, is ridiculous!"

Morlanna raised an eyebrow, knowing he couldn't fire her for such an innocent infraction. "Sir, I am asking for the opportunity to either prove or disprove the stories coming from the Texas papers. If they are false, you have a story proving the nonsense of a growing religion as you have called it."

He walked across the office and looked out a window. "So, you're using my own words against me." Ludsworth struck a match on the windowsill, relighting his cigar. "I never approved of you being here. The work of reporting and writing the news is a man's business. Women have no place in it."

"I know exactly where women belong in your world," she thought.

"You were clever using your middle name and fooling me into hiring you."

She wished to smile but withheld it. "Lynn is such an ambiguous little name, don't you agree? I do appreciate you making the offer of employment in writing. It kept things straightforward, avoiding the need for lawyers. It would have been an ugly court scene replayed multiple times in the newspapers if you refused to fulfill a legal and binding contract."

He whipped around and pointed the cigar at her. "You think you're pretty smart, don't you? I have regretted my decision every day since you walked through the doors of my office. Alright, go, write your story. I still have the option of printing it. There will not be one extra dime from the paper for this adventure except your salary. God knows I don't need anyone thinking I believe in these smoke and mirror charades."

She rose, straightening the brown and tan striped blouse, then smiled at him. "I do not need your money."

His face turned a reddish-purple. "Get out! Go find your ghost!"

"I should be back in six to eight weeks," she said and turned her back to him.

"Take forever, your absence will be a relief from the constant irritation you cause me daily."

The sound of her skirt and the click of heels were methodical as Morlanna exited the large office. She walked out into a smoke-filled floor of men and machines, moving quickly to her desk. She opened the middle drawer removing the train tickets to Texas and Louisiana.

"Excuse me, are you Miss Miller?"

She looked down at a young boy dressed in short pants, a shirt, and a cap. "Yes, do you have business with me, young sir?"

The boy blushed, quickly removing his cap. "I have a telegram for you," he said handing her the envelope and turning to leave.

"Just a moment. What's your name?" she asked.

The boy stopped turning back. "James, Miss."

Morlanna took a seat at the desk and reached for her purse pulling out fifty cents. "Mr. James, thank you for bringing this." She watched as his eyes widened at the tip, and then motioned for him to move closer. "Place these coins in your pocket and do not tell anyone," she said, winking at him.

"Yes, Miss, I won't tell no one, thank you," he said and hurried out of the building.

"You make us all look like vile scrooges tipping that little street runner, Morlanna," a male voice said over her shoulder.

"All of you are scrooges, Wilson." She stood up and faced the tall, handsome, well-dressed man. "These children should be in school learning to read and write, not work on the streets or dying in factories."

"Always thinking of the less fortunate. Odd since some of your family built its wealth on exploiting them," he said, instantly regretting the comment.

She raised her skirt in one quick move and kicked him hard on the shin. "Maybe you should think about who exploits the street whores." Her voice raised several octaves and caused everyone on the news floor to stop working and stare at them.

He leaned over in pain. "I'm sorry."

"Yes, you are. Excuse me. I have an assignment."

Wilson rubbed his shin and snickered. He looked around the room at everyone and raised a hand. "Everything is fine. A simple disagreement on the political climate of the city." He leaned closer to her. "Ghost hunting, I understand. Be careful, Morlanna, they might keep you."

"What a pity, you'll be reduced to degrading the flower ladies and street vendors instead of me."

"Morlanna."

"Goodbye, Wilson," she said, taking the train tickets and telegram placing them in her purse. She pinned a tan-colored hat in the upswept hair and pulled the veil over her face.

As she reached for her coat, Wilson removed it from the stand, waiting for a reaction. She backed into the jacket, refusing to give him further attention.

He took her arm. "At least let me buy you dinner, and allow me the opportunity to make amends."

She pulled away gently. "I'm afraid there isn't enough wine in the city to make amends for your actions today." Morlanna picked up her belongings and walked away.

In a few weeks, she would prove women were equals with men in reporting the news for a reading world.

Chapter 3

Sabotage

Wilson Derby watched as Morlanna defiantly walked off the main floor of the newspaper, moving to the window in time to see her wave for the streetcar. The five-foot-two-inch spitfire brandished a temper to match her red hair and emerald eyes. His fascination with her began the first day she entered the building. The woman oozed confidence and a large amount of bravery. His charming swagger at six foot one, dark brown hair, and eyes did not impress the lady.

The woman insulted his manhood on more than one occasion in the office since arriving. It took a year before she accepted a request to join him for an evening out. The night ended with a public scene when a lady of the evening approached him on the street.

"So, you're too good for me now, taking up with the high-class ladies," she said, pointing to Morlanna.

Wilson took a protective stance. "Be on your way, harlot. You insult good and decent people."

The woman stepped back and laughed. "Harlot? I'll remember your words when you come searching for me later tonight, once you had your fun with the uppity bitch."

Wilson held up his cane. "Be gone or I'll call for the police." Waiting until the woman disappeared around the corner, he turned back to apologize for the interruption. Morlanna was entering a carriage taxi half a street away. As he ran up to the door intending to join her, a hand reached out the window throwing money on the ground. He backed away as the carriage left.

Any conversation between them now took place on the work floor. Familiar footsteps walked up behind him.

"Derby, a moment of your time in my office. You may want to bring that notebook of yours. I have some information you will need to remember," Ludsworth said.

"Yes, sir," he said and followed behind like a puppy as everyone in the office did, except Morlanna.

Ludsworth shut the door behind them. "Take a seat."

Wilson glanced at the uncomfortable chair. "If you don't mind, I'd prefer to stand. I bumped my shin earlier and sitting would irritate it further."

"Yes, I saw the accident with Miss Miller's boot. Now, sit down."

Wilson moved to the chair. "Is there a problem, sir?"

Ludsworth lit a new cigar taking his place behind the desk. "I have something you need to do for me."

"I hope it's a story on a dirty politician."

Ludsworth raised his head and blew smoke toward the ceiling. "I wish it was that simple." He took two tickets from his coat pocket, placed them on top of an envelope, and pushed it across the desk. "I want you to follow that little redhead and make sure she doesn't embarrass the newspaper."

Wilson took a moment to view the tickets grimacing at the final location. "I'm not sure you've chosen the right person, sir."

Ludsworth leaned across the desk. "Oh, I believe I have chosen the perfect person. What's the problem, are you afraid of ghosts?"

Wilson could feel his face turning red. "Of course not, there is no such thing. Dead is dead. Where is this town located?"

Ludsworth handed Wilson Morlanna's file. "According to her file, somewhere between Calcasieu and Cameron Parish. I discovered what she was researching months ago and knew where it would eventually lead. We need to get ahead of her and stop the madness of all these occult beliefs. There's enough money in the other envelope for a month of provisions, and I've arranged for your lodging. Make sure you read the information in her file."

"Why?"

"I hoped you might try and do some work instead of everything always being handed to you," Ludsworth told him.

"Handed? In what manner?"

"The story of the mayor embezzling city funds came from his wife. You were sleeping with her at the time, as I remember. Wasn't it one of your street whores who gave you information on the police chief's social disease?"

Wilson stopped counting the money and raised his head. "There's no need to be insulting."

Ludsworth could see Wilson salivating over the money. "If you spend everything, there will be no more, understood?"

"Of course, what type of lodging arrangements require provisions?"

"I suggest you brush up on your cooking skills as you will not be staying in town, it's too risky. A man named Leotis Guidry will meet you at your destination. He owns the general store and is the center for all information in the town and surrounding area. I received a telegram from him advising Miss Miller will be staying at Ms. Elsie's boarding house."

Wilson began feeling ill. "Can you explain my assignment?"

"First, keep out of sight, find the Bishop's Palace, and do whatever is necessary to see she has no story to write. I'll take great pleasure in firing her for failure to complete the assignment."

"I'll leave a few days after she does."

"No! You're on the first train leaving in the morning. There doesn't need to be two strangers running around the town asking questions. I suggest you leave your fancy clothes here. You will need to blend in with the locals not stand out like a clown."

"How do you expect me to manage that?"

A grin spread across his face. "You'll find out in a few days, now go home and pack a small bag."

Wilson stood up, placing the envelope in his pants pocket. "I won't let you down, sir."

Ludsworth raised a hand and motioned for him to leave.

As Wilson left the office, he couldn't understand why this mess should involve him? He ran a hand through his hair, thinking the easy life would be changing shortly to something foreign and unpleasant. The streets all began to look the same as he wandered through them stopping when the city workers began lighting the lamps along his path. Wilson leaned against a building, hiding in the shadows to light a cigarette. He shook his head knowing for the first time, in his twenty-eight years, there would be no one to rescue him.

He looked across the street at the figure sitting in the window smoking. Morlanna was responsible for his current situation. She enjoyed a good chase for a story regardless of the location or trouble it might incur. He preferred a structured, straight-line objective to a story without working for it. Hopefully, this job would be simple and financially rewarding when he returned.

He crushed the cigarette on the brick wall and then opened her file, scanning through a few pages. "Trash."

A few blocks away, he struck a match setting the file ablaze, dropping it in a refuse bin.

Chapter 4

Morlanna left the newspaper and went directly back to the house where she rented a small upstairs room. She stopped and knocked on the landlord's door, smiling at the memory of their first meeting. The Montgomerys were a lovely couple in their late sixties and hesitant in the beginning to rent a single woman the room. It took two afternoons of drinking tea and eating cakes to convince them her intentions were honorable.

The handwritten and detailed restrictions Mrs. Montgomery presented when she moved in were amusing. "No male visitors" had been printed in large letters and underlined twice. The local churches were listed according to beliefs and included Sunday service times. The wickedness of tobacco and alcohol were explained in a church tract, and forbidden inside the house.

Morlanna might have declined the rental if the determination to be an independent woman and reporter wasn't so important. Her father wanted to help with finances, but she refused determined to do this alone. He set up a small account in one of the banks sending a small allowance should the need arise. She lived minimally on the salary from the newspaper and the opportunity to be acknowledged for her work would be worth the inconvenience.

The door opened. "Good day, Mrs. Montgomery. I need to speak with you and your husband.

A small woman with grey hair pulled back in a tight bun greeted her. "Is there a problem Miss Miller?"

"No, I am going on an assignment for the paper and wish to pay my rent early."

Mrs. Montgomery stepped out of the doorway in a cream-colored dress and brown apron. "Come in, dear. I'll put on the kettle."

"I'd love a cup of tea, thank you," Morlanna told her.

She followed the small woman into the kitchen and sat down at the table near a small bay window. Mr. Montgomery entered the back door holding a bouquet.

"Good afternoon, Miss Miller," he said and then handed the lavender daisies and yellow buttercups to his wife. "It's always nice having our star boarder visit."

"Miss Miller is going on an assignment and wished to pay ahead on her rent."

"An assignment?" he asked.

"Yes, I cannot say much about it for now," Morlanna explained.

"Well, I guess we will just have to wait and read about it in the paper once you have written the story," he stated.

"I'm sure it will be interesting. How long will you be gone, dear?" Mrs. Montgomery asked.

"At least four maybe six weeks. I would like to pay for two months in advance."

Morlanna could see the couple seemed surprised at the amount of time she would be gone.

"You are coming back?" Mrs. Montgomery asked, concerned.

She smiled and touched the woman's hand. "I assure you nothing will keep me from returning. If I am delayed for any reason, I will send word."

Mrs. Montgomery placed a pot of tea and three cups on the table.

"When will you be leaving?" he asked.

Morlanna placed a teaspoon of sugar in her cup and a small amount of milk. "In two days."

"We will be anxious to hear all about your experience when you return," Mrs. Montgomery told her.

Morlanna settled into the chair knowing the next two hours would be spent listening to all the neighborhood gossip and Mr. Montgomery's gardening adventures.

"It has been a pleasure as always visiting, but I should go up and start preparing for my trip," she said.

"If there is anything we can do, please let us know," Mr. Montgomery told her.

"I will," she said, walking upstairs to her room.

Once the door was closed, she removed the work clothes, stripping down to undergarments and covering herself with a sheer robe. She stared at the corset on a chair wondering why women exchanged one torture for another in the name of progress? At least the flat-back skirts were comfortable compared to the ungiving bustles of a few years ago.

She opened the windows allowing a breeze into the room and took time to properly read the telegram delivered to the office. The Montgomerys' had been specific on many things of propriety in reference to smoking. The green glass atomizer filled with mint water and leaving a window open helped keep her habit a secret. The cool night air and a cigarette were a nice relief from the stress of work. She removed the telegram from the envelope and smiled at the response from the boarding house. Ms. Elsie would be happy to have her as a guest. Morlanna laughed at the small addendum, stating all boarders would be expected to follow the rules. "Rules" were in capital letters.

She glanced at the work notebook lying on the small table. Wilson gave it to her as a gift the only night they went out together. Morlanna wondered if he kept work-related information in his or a list of conquests and liaisons. This trip to Louisiana would possibly lead to the truth about all the disappearances in a small town. She read over the notes from witness statements who swore on the souls of family members evil lived and walked the streets nightly. Ghouls and ghosts danced in the cemetery, while a demon priest stole the souls of those daring to enter his home in search of treasure. Chaste men disappeared, never returning to family or friends. She thought it seemed odd there were no stories of women missing and planned to prove these were stories for children and the weak-minded.

She knew there were usually simple explanations in all legends. The so-called chaste men probably wished to escape the responsibilities of wives or lovers. It's easier to say the devil took them than admit the truth. Ludsworth's comment about smoke and mirrors was the correct answer to the occult, all she needed to do is prove it. Morlanna stopped believing in spirits and demons once her grandmother died.

As she closed the window the glimpse of a fire in a refuse bin up the street caught her attention. "What fool did that?"

Chapter 5

Monday, September 1st
   Early morning

Morlanna folded the letter and slipped it into an envelope, addressing it to her family. An explanation for a lengthy absence would be necessary to avoid her father sending out a search party. Unfavorable weather delayed this trip, but instead of brooding, she spent time researching in the city library. The discovery of additional material surrounding the palace included folklore, stories of Voodoo priestesses, and the demon bishop. The area of Louisiana she intended to visit appeared extremely interesting, at least in print.

She sent a telegram, to Ms. Elsie, with an explanation of the later arrival date. The promise of additional compensation to continue holding the room prompted a rapid and positive response. The creaking boards made by heavy footsteps caused her head to rise and check the time. The individuals she hired for transportation to the train station were early, which pleased her. A light knock on the door made her pat the derringer in the dress pocket. The words of a military father took Morlanna back to the first day of firearms training, she was six years old.

"I'll not have a daughter afraid of her shadow or defenseless."

She opened the door. "Good morning."

The two men quickly removed their caps, viewing her. "Good morning, Miss."

"I have one item," she replied, pointing across the room at the travel trunk standing by the bed.

"Begging your pardon Miss, we didn't come in a carriage," the older man said.

"I'm aware of the transportation I ordered. The wagon will be acceptable for the short ride to the train station. Please come in," she said and stepped out of the doorway.

"At your service," the older man said. He motioned for the younger man to enter. "We'll be on the street waiting for you, Miss." They replaced their caps and picked up the trunk.

"Your name, sir."

"Orson, Miss, and my son, Lewis."

"It's a pleasure. I have a letter to post on the way."

He motioned toward his son. "Lewis will do it for you if it's your wish."

"Thank you, I'll be down shortly," she said, closing the door as they exited.

She spent the next few moments checking the apartment before pinning a small black hat in her hair. A black and white striped jacket was buttoned over a white blouse and black skirt, making her frown at the uncomfortable travel clothes. She picked up the small leather travel bag and black drawstring purse from the bed, tucking the letter in her pocket with her gun.

She locked the door and descended the stairs to the sight of Mrs. Montgomery holding a small cloth bag and dabbing her eyes.

"I thought you might like something since it's so early," she said, handing the bag to Morlanna.

She took a moment peeking inside. "Fresh biscuits and jam will be the perfect companion, thank you. I'll send word should my trip be extended."

"Take care, dear."

She took the woman's hand and squeezed it before leaving the house. The older man waited at the wagon and assisted her into the front seat. The night skies were beginning to change and hung between night and day. She compared this time to the catholic belief in purgatory, neither day nor night, heaven or hell.

"My apologies again, Miss," Orson said and joined her in the front seat.

"No need for apologies, this isn't my first experience in a wagon," she said, placing on a pair of black leather gloves. "I'd like a chance at the reins, with your permission."

The older man took a moment staring at her, then passed the reins. "Sally, on the left, likes to lead so give her a little more slack."

Morlanna nodded and motioned for him to release the brake. "Get up!"

The handling of a team brought sweet memories of her teenage years. She stopped the wagon in front of the station, causing a few individuals to stare and point at the spectacle.

"It appears a few disapprove of my driving," she said.

"I don't rightly believe you give a care," Orson said, laughing as he helped her down.

Morlanna watched as he assisted his son with the trunk, calling for the porter. She reached inside the skirt pocket and removed the letter. "Let me give you money for the postage."

Lewis removed his cap, holding a hand up to stop her from giving him more money. "I'll see to your letter once we leave. Have a nice trip, Miss."

She closed her purse and nodded. "You have a good man there."

Orson glanced toward Lewis. "I try my best. Safe journey, Miss."

She reached out to shake hands, leaving a tip in Orson's'. Morlanna turned around to the porter waiting for instructions.

"I'd like this available and not stored." She handed him her ticket.

He took a moment to check the exact location of the private coach. "Yes Miss, please, follow me."

They walked across the station platform and to the back of the train, where she entered a private coach. The sitting room held two chairs with a small dining table for meals. The bedroom seemed comfortable and included a private lavatory. She tipped the porter locking the outside door behind him. The knock on the door leading into the hallway meant the conductor had arrived.

The man tipped his cap. "Your ticket."

She presented her ticket and waited as he glanced around the room. "Is there a problem?"

He looked at her, raising an eyebrow. "No, your ticket is in order. I'll send an attendant after we're on our way."

Morlanna closed the door, annoyed with the actions of the conductor. At twenty-five, some considered her a spinster though the average age for women to be married was twenty-two. One day opinions would change on single women choosing a career over early marriage. She entered the main room and removed the jacket and hat, throwing them on the nearest chair. The smell of cigars and cigarettes clung to the curtains bringing a smile, as this meant smoking inside would be permissible. The sound of the whistle indicated those still on the platform should move inside or be left behind. She walked out the back door onto the small platform and stood at the railing. As the train pulled away from the station, an icy chill ran down her back. She pushed it away, blaming the morning breeze and thrill of the adventure ahead.

Chapter 6

Tuesday, September 2nd

Wilson opened his eyes to the sudden crowing of a rooster. As he shifted slightly the shooting pain in his back and legs brought a realization of the current situation. The four-to-five hour trip wasn't something he expected on the back of a demon, nor the rutted roads. The ability to sit or stand comfortably would be questionable, making his assignment in danger of failing. The rooster crowed again and again.

"Shut up! Shut up! Shut Up!"

The animal outside the door ignored his demands. He squinted as the sun began shining through the small window covered with a piece of thin tattered material. A bead of sweat ran down the left side of his face into his ear. He quickly wiped the rest away and looked at the dirty ceiling.

"Ludsworth, you worthless bastard. If I don't die in this place, I promise you will pay for every moment of pain endured."

He should have known this trip was doomed when the conductor showed him to the coach section of the train. A quick slip of cash into the man's palm moved him into a small individual berth. This allowed access to the private dining car where he had the good fortune of meeting a lovely lady. He smiled and took a deep breath hoping to smell her sweet perfume.

The odor of chickens and animal excrement filled his nose, forcing a gagging reflex. The sudden change in position sent a searing pain through his body and forced him to grab the sides of the bed. He couldn't understand why his final destination consisted of riding on the back of a demon instead of arriving directly in town.

"Bonjour" A jovial male voice said.

Wilson turned toward the door shaking his head.

Leotis grinned. "I'm sorry, good morning."

He looked at the figure in the door. Leotis Guidry appeared to be forty years old, medium build, with black hair and dark eyes. The Louisiana sun tanned his skin a leathery brown. He held a pitcher of water, a towel, and a small jar.

"I beg to differ, sir," he said, grimacing with each movement.

He laughed. "You must rise, and move or the pain will take longer to go away. I brought freshwater, something for your discomfort, and a telegram."

Wilson gingerly began to move and cursed with every inch. He positioned himself facing Leotis. "I have a question."

"I will answer it if I can," Leotis said.

"Why in the name of God was I not sent directly here?"

"Strangers arriving in our small town do not go unnoticed. Mr. Ludsworth and I agreed that you should not arrive here. He failed to inform me you did not ride well or I would have brought a wagon."

Wilson reached out taking the items from Leotis and placed them on the bed. He held up the jar. "What's this?"

"A salve for horses," Leotis answered.

"Horses."

"It will help the soreness."

"Horses," Wilson repeated.

He laughed. "There is food inside my home when you are ready."

"Horses."

Leotis waved a hand and left the small building.

Wilson scanned the place he would call home for a few weeks. It wasn't more than a shed with a small handmade bed, a table and chair, no lavatory, running water, or stove, not that he needed it in the ungodly swelter. He barely remembered Leotis pointing toward the outhouse yesterday as they arrived before sundown. He took a breath and stood up, moving slowly out the door with the jar of horse liniment.

"Watch out for snakes!" Leotis bellowed from the back door of the house.

Once his personal business had been completed, Wilson walked toward the house and noticed he felt less discomfort. He couldn't be sure if the salve or action of rubbing the tender areas helped.

Leotis saw him walking toward the house and opened the door. "Café?"

"Yes, please." Wilson accepted the cup of steaming black coffee and then glanced around the small kitchen focusing on the straight-back wooden chairs around the table. "I think I'll stand for now."

Laughter filled the kitchen. "Chéri, we have company."

A small woman with dark brown hair and eyes entered the kitchen, wearing a dress covered with blue flowers and a yellow apron. She took a pan from the cookstove oven and placed food on a plate giving it to Leotis. He handed the food and a fork to Wilson.

"This smells excellent," Wilson said and set the coffee cup on the table.

A conversation began between Leotis and the woman. The whispered words quickly increased to harsh strong tones ending with a wave of his hand toward her. She turned to stare at Wilson, crossing herself before leaving the kitchen.

Wilson took a bite of food and looked at Leotis, "Problem?"

"My wife, Cecile, is superstitious. In the bayous and swamps of Louisiana, there are stories we cannot easily explain to outsiders. The Rougarou, Grunch, Lutin, and even Witches are often used to keep children from disobeying parents or wandering too far from the house at night." He pointed toward the crucifixes in the kitchen. "She believes you will bring evil into our home."

Wilson handed his empty plate to Leotis and picked up the coffee cup. "I don't believe in scary stories which frighten children."

"You would be wise to listen and not dismiss our beliefs."

Wilson snickered. "Who can tell me about the palace?"

"You will need to talk with people closer to the swamps."

"What about in town?" Wilson asked.

"You should stay away. I will bring any information from those coming to my store should it be mentioned."

"I hoped you might be able to give me directions," Wilson said.

Leotis shook his head. "There are people in the parish that know its location."

"I can't believe Ludsworth sent me here to look for an abandoned building. It's probably a pile of rubble due to this God-forsaken humidity with rats and mice running through it."

Leotis poured more coffee for them and motioned for Wilson to follow him outside. "Cecile does not allow talk of the palace inside the house."

Wilson could not believe he was going outside with this swamp dweller who believed in monsters to have a conversation. He watched as Leotis took a few moments scanning the area before speaking.

"You're afraid, aren't you?" Wilson asked.

"Try to understand, some of our stories are based on part truth, others myth and legend. The Bishop's Palace is more truth than a fable."

"Sir, it is just a building."

"No, it is not. It began as a simple home for a man of God. When the priest died, the town offered the bishop a wealth of treasure to stay and take his place. The bishop agreed and demanded a grand home be built for him. Over time he betrayed God and the people."

"What happened?"

"When the people refused to give him more treasure, he made a bargain with the devil for power and wealth,"

"I assume the bargain included some type of payment?"

"Souls," Leotis answered.

Wilson shook his head. "Are you saying there is gold inside the palace?"

"Yes."

Wilson began smiling. "Well, this has taken a pleasant turn to my dilemma."

"Men are blinded by riches and forget there is always a price to pay."

"You're telling me the devil gave the priest gold so he could lure men inside and take their souls," Wilson said.

Leotis dropped his head. "Bishop, not priest, and you've been warned. If you do learn of its location, no one will accompany you to the palace."

"I must locate it and go inside at least once."

"Better you go back alive," Leotis said.

Wilson handed his coffee cup to Leotis. "Treasure, you say? Sounds too good to miss out on leaving here rich."

"You enter the palace at your peril," Leotis said.

Laughing. "Thanks for the story. I don't believe in such nonsense. Do you know of anyone who found gold or silver and lived?"

"Only one."

"Can I speak with him or her," Wilson said.

"It isn't possible."

"Why?"

"He could no longer speak after returning from the palace," Leotis said and looked back toward his home.

"Convenient, another local story no way to prove," he turned and walked away from Leotis.

"Fool!" Leotis said and reached in his pocket, removing a coin. His brother had taken pirate's gold from the Bishop's Palace, paying a terrible price.

Wilson heard Leotis mumbling as he walked away to try and freshen himself outside in the hot Louisiana sun. The water did little to relieve his discomfort or remove the smell of excrement. Wilson re-entered the shed discovering a package under the bed. He opened the paper wrappings.

"Wonderful."

Overalls, shirts, pants, a jacket, and a cap lay in his lap with a pair of brown high boots at the bottom of the clothes. He looked down at his clothes covered in dust and sweat. Wilson cursed Ludsworth again, realizing the days ahead would be uncomfortable but mostly undignified for a man of his status. Thankfully, no one would ever see him dressed as a country bumpkin. He picked up the telegram left on the bed earlier and opened it.

Miss Miller delayed, departed 1, September. (STOP)
Take advantage of your time, before her arrival. (STOP)
You won't get another chance. (STOP)
Ludsworth.

Morlanna would arrive in approximately a week by train and check in to the boarding house. He needed to complete his investigation and keep out of town. The final step would be to locate the palace and search for anything of value, take it, then destroy anything standing.

The stories of treasure seemed a mainstay in folklore, and the palace would probably be no different. He shivered at the thought of discovering such wealth. The newspaper would run a story of his success, elevating him into high society. He would no longer require the money of old women longing for his company. Wilson's time and attention would be given to the high-priced whores he preferred.

He smiled and thought of Morlanna returning with no proof or story to write. Ludsworth would focus his full wrath and degradation on her as a failed reporter in front of everyone on the work floor. Her embarrassing dismissal would be small compensation for all he endured in the swamps.

Wilson rubbed his face feeling stubble. "Maybe I'll grow a beard."

Chapter 7

Wednesday, September 10th
　Change of Plan

Wilson discovered the continued use of horse salve and physical activity did help the pain to subside over the week. He jotted down the name of the ointment in his notebook should the need ever arise again for overused muscle discomfort. He managed to mount the horse the next morning and begin his investigation.

The warning Leotis gave about the locals seemed outlandish but proved factual. The only thing that encouraged people to talk when it came to the Bishop's Palace seemed to be money or liquor. He received little or no information on the location of the Bishop's Palace or any of the missing individuals. One man told him the Bishop's Palace was a rite of passage for the youth in the area. No one would admit to going inside or knowing the names of those who did. The story remained the same, a Catholic Bishop denied God and made a pact with the devil, who lavished him with silver and gold for the souls of men.

He disliked relying on Leotis for information in town, but the last thing Ludsworth needed would be for Morlanna to discover their plan to discredit her. His scruffy appearance and clothing didn't fool anyone, they still saw him as a stranger asking too many questions.

Wilson returned to the farm after another day of no new information and discovered Leotis waiting for him outside the shed. "What can I do for you?"

"Thought I should stop by and see how things are going for you."

Wilson shrugged his shoulders. "You were right. It's been difficult, no that isn't right, it's been impossible to obtain the location of the palace."

"I tried explaining how folks are in the parish. Some believe even mentioning the location or the bishop will bring misfortune inside their home. I stopped by the boarding house today, and there has been a further delay on her boarder coming from California."

"Did she happen to say how long a delay?" Wilson inquired.

"She'll be arriving Saturday. I suggest whatever you intend to do should be completed soon. Folks around the parish are asking questions about the odd-looking stranger."

He rubbed his face. "I never expected this ruse would work, though I have grown fond of the beard. It may make the ladies adore me, even more, when I return to San Francisco."

"Be cautious who you speak with over the next few days. My store is not the only place in town where people gather to spread gossip."

"I assume the boarding house is one of those places. I've heard a couple of stories about Ms. Elsie," Wilson said.

"She is a good woman."

"But."

"Ms. Elsie has dealings with a Voodoo priestess. She claims holiness on Sunday taking communion, then holds backroom seances during the week in her home."

Wilson raised his head toward the sky. "The one person in town I could charm for information stopped by someone not even here."

"What is your plan?" Leotis asked.

"The one I've had since arriving here, find the palace and take a serious look at this house of evil. Once I'm satisfied there is nothing of value in all the stories, I'll leave the stench of chickens and swamp behind. What is so damn important about a pile of stones that no one will give up its location?"

Leotis shook his head. "It is not. The palace has never changed, it remains as it was the day workers set the last stone."

Wilson took a moment to realize what Leotis said to him. "You worthless son-of-a-bitch. You know where the palace is, don't you? You let me run all over the area in this damn heat, asking questions no one would answer, why?"

"Wilson, you must understand," Leotis stated.

"Understand what? That you have made a fool of me?"

"No. The Bishop's Palace is a place of evil. We have sworn as a community to keep strangers from discovering its location."

"What you mean is the community is perpetuating a lie."

"Have you not listened to anything the people have told you about the palace?"

"A well-rehearsed story, it seems," Wilson told him.

"We hoped you would become frustrated and leave with no one giving up its location. Everything I have told you is true."

"Then you can take me to the palace so I can see for myself."

"I will not take you, but I will draw a map of its location," Leotis told him.

Wilson tore a page from his notebook and handed him the paper and a pencil. "Make the directions clear and easy to follow."

Leotis took a few minutes drawing out the area and road leading to the palace. He handed it to Wilson. "Do not go there after dark."

"Please stop, I am not a child." Wilson looked at the drawing. "What is this?"

"The cemetery you must pass through to get to the palace."

"Where is the road?"

"Destroyed by storms, never rebuilt in the hope it would keep people away. The Bishop's Palace was built between 1817 and 1818, the only way to it now is through the cemetery. There are no longer fresh flowers brought to the dead, the grass will not grow, and thick vines will block your way. The fence that surrounds the cemetery never weathers or ages like the palace," Leotis said.

"A decrepit unkept graveyard to weave through and more lies." Wilson closed his eyes and sighed, wishing he could be anywhere else but here. "Please send a telegram advising Mr. Ludsworth I'll be leaving before Miss Miller arrives with the information he requested."

"When will you go out to the palace?"

"I will go first thing tomorrow morning in the light of day as you suggested. Once I've searched the building, I'll leave-taking the first train out Friday."

Leotis stood for a moment staring at him. "I do not believe you. Men like you are never satisfied with words." He reached in his pocket and flipped the gold coin toward Wilson.

He caught it, entranced by the gold gleaming in the sunlight. "Where did you get this?"

"From my brother, the only person to ever escape the palace. He never spoke another word and suffered terrible fits after returning."

"Can I speak with him?"

Leotis shook his head. "Passed."

Wilson held the coin out. "You should keep it."

Leotis shook his head. "When you see the devil, give it back to him. If you should make it out of the palace alive leave the horse at the livery. I'll pick him up on my way home," he told Wilson and walked away.

Wilson smiled and flipped the gold coin over in his hand. The stories of treasure were true. He knew Leotis didn't believe he would wait until daylight, but it didn't matter since he had no intentions of ever returning to this part of the world. He entered the shed and looked in the corner where his city clothes lay on the dirt floor, ruined. They would be left with the rest of his unpleasant memories.

If the palace truly stood, he would use the kerosene he borrowed from Leotis to destroy anything of importance for Morlanna's story. In the morning, word of the tragic destruction of the Bishop's Palace would be the topic of conversation in town. He would triumphantly return to San Francisco with a great trophy that would mean never-ending stories at Ludsworth's private club. Wilson would be treated to endless glasses of whiskey as he repeated the bravery and skill it took to steal the coin from the hand of Satan.

Wilson placed the leather notebook, the money still left that Ludsworth gave him, and the gold coin on the small table. He took time to make another copy of the map, placing it inside the book. At dusk, he left the property heading out on a final quest. The map turned out to be simple to follow, and his destination achieved when the horse refused to move forward. After securing the animal to a small tree limb, he took the two cans of kerosene and walked toward a stand of trees. The discovery of a well-worn path instead of tall grass and weeds to trudge through indicated someone visited the area regularly. He raised the lantern arriving at the back gate of the cemetery, then stepped forward to inspect the iron. It appeared strong and practically new, with the smell of fresh paint lingering in the air.

He exited out the front gate of the graveyard and stopped, captivated at the splendor of the Bishop's Palace. This confirmed in his mind the existence of a resident. The glowing lanterns in multiple windows and smoke billowing from two chimneys were inviting. The warmth emanating from the palace ceased any thought of danger to himself. He left the cans of kerosene behind and moved forward mesmerized by the architecture. The multiple turrets gave a regal appearance drawing him closer, where he discovered marble door frames inlaid with gold.

A feeling of embarrassment overwhelmed him due to his shabby and unkempt appearance. The resident of this magnificent home would be a man or woman of substance and would expect a gentleman to be appropriately dressed for an evening visit. The feeling of inadequacy faded as his right hand reached for the door knocker giving one tap. Wilson could feel his heart racing as he waited to be received. The doors opened wide with a glow that beckoned him to enter.

He bowed to the man standing at the door. "Wilson Derby of San Francisco, representing Mr. Milford Ludsworth, and the *Worth Daily News*."

"Ah, Mister Derby, please come in. I've been waiting for you."

Chapter 8

Thursday, September 11th

Cecile stood outside feeding the chickens when the site of their horse grazing in the yard caught her attention. She remembered Leotis saying Wilson would be using the horse today, but it was thoughtless of him to allow the animal to roam free instead of being corralled. A cold chill ran over her as she glanced toward the small building where no signs of life appeared. There had been troubling signs this morning, no eggs in the coop, a bird in the house, and now a horse with no rider.

She walked slowly toward the small building calling out. "Monsieur Derby." No answer. She called again, "Monsieur Derby, are you alright?"

A hand touched her shoulder. Cecile dropped the feed pan screaming. "Holy Mother of God, save me."

"Chéri, what's wrong?"

Cecile placed both hands over her face. "Trouble is upon us," she said and pointed toward the horse.

Leotis smiled, pulling her into him. "Wilson is taking the horse later. It broke away to feed, nothing more."

She shook her head at him. "No. I have seen the signs, Leotis. The hens did not lay, there are always eggs in the morning, and a bird flew into the house. The signs have spoken misfortune is coming to our home."

He patted her on the back and kissed her forehead. "Chéri, don't worry. Go inside make some café for us. I'll check on Wilson and the horse. You will see all is well."

She nodded, picking up the pan, and headed toward the house. Cecile watched from the door as Leotis entered the shed. He wasn't inside long before he left to retrieve the horse from the field. When her husband removed the saddle and placed the horse in the corral, she stepped away from the door.

Leotis entered the back door, handing her two eggs. Cecille's hands were shaking when she took them and placed them in a basket.

"Monsieur Derby?"

He shook his head. "The bed has not been slept in, and his city clothes are on the floor. The notebook he writes in and money are on the table."

"What about the animal?"

"There was a small branch in the reins, the animal easily broke free returning home."

She crossed herself and whispered a short prayer. "The devil has taken him."

"Cecile, we do not know this for sure. He would not leave his belongings or this," he said, removing the gold coin from his pocket.

"You gave him your coin?"

"I told him to give it back to the devil, hoping it would keep him away from the palace."

She walked over, placing a hand on his arm. "In the palace, he will have no need for such things. We must burn his possessions and rid our home of this evil."

He wrapped his arms around her. "We will leave them for now. If he does not return, I will remove them."

She nodded. "Leotis, no more strangers in our home, promise me."

Nodding. "No more strangers. I swear it."

Chapter 9

Morlanna could not have been more relieved to be in the bright sunshine and on steady ground as the train pulled into the station. She placed her hat and jacket on, waiting for the conductor to open the door to her private coach. He brought a porter with him to take her trunk to the platform. After leaving the train, it took a few moments for her footing to be stable and not sway. They walked through the station and out the front entrance, where she tipped the porter. The dry streets were a welcome change from the muck and mud of Houston.

"Miss Miller."

She looked up to see a man holding his cap. "Yes."

"I am Leotis Guidry. I'll be escorting you to Ms. Elsie's."

"Splendid, I have one trunk."

"I'll see to it. My wagon is to your left," he told her.

"Is it far to the boarding house?"

He smiled. "No, the location is on the opposite side of town. A little far to carry a trunk."

They walked to the wagon, where Leotis assisted her to the seat. He drove through the town filled with people going about their Saturday business. As they arrived, she thought this house may have been part of a larger farm at one time due to its size and location at the end of the town. After Mr. Guidry helped her out of the wagon, she walked up the stairs and knocked on the door. A woman in her fifties answered the door, dressed in black from head to toe. She began to smile, realizing her boarder had arrived.

She opened the door. "Miss Miller, child, please come in. I have been worried about you and all the dreadful weather in Texas."

"Yes, an unpleasant experience, but I am happy to be where the sun is shining and the ground dry."

Elsie looked at Leotis. "Mr. Guidry, will you take Miss Miller's belongings upstairs to room three, the door is unlocked."

"Yes, Ms. Elsie."

"Miss Miller, I have some information on the town and my rules for the boarding house. Can I offer you a cup of tea?"

"Tea would be lovely," she said and followed the woman into the parlor.

"Of course, dear. I'll set the kettle."

Morlanna smiled as the woman walked away and moved back to the entry hearing the footsteps of Mr. Guidry. "Thank you," she said and handed him money.

He nodded taking the coins, then stepped into the parlor door, turning back. "Be cautious in this house."

She tilted her head. "I will, sir."

"Good day," he said and left.

"Miss Miller, I have your tea."

She entered the parlor and took a seat, enjoying the refreshments. "This tea is perfect after such a disagreeable trip."

Ms. Elsie reached over patting Morlanna's hand, and gave her several pieces of paper. "Well, all that is in the past."

"Would it be permissible to take these upstairs?"

She nodded. "Of course, I need a little information for my records, no hurry." Ms. Elsie hesitated a moment. "I do not wish to be impolite, but I have held your room for some time."

Morlanna opened her purse, taking out several bills. "Thank you for being agreeable to my delay. I don't wish to be rude, but it's been a long trip."

"I understand, you should rest."

"Ms. Elsie, do you know if there a laundress in town? I'm afraid most of my clothes are in dire need of cleaning and repair."

"I know the perfect person, Mr. Guidry's wife. I'll be happy to take your clothes and drop them off at his store. Cecile should have them back to you in a few days."

"He has a store?"

"The local feed store, though now it's more of a general store. He has everything from feed to personal needs."

"I accept your offer, but would prefer to pick them up so I can pay for the work. It will be nice to acquaint myself with the town."

"As you wish. Would you like dinner in your room tonight?"

"No, I'll come downstairs. What time?" Morlanna asked.

"I'm having a few friends over this evening and dinner will be at six."

"I'll be prompt," she said.

"I'll show you to your room," Elsie said.

Morlanna followed the woman upstairs, touring the lavatory, and waited as Ms. Elsie opened the door to her room.

"Do you have a key for me?"

Ms. Elsie seemed surprised. "I have the only key to these rooms. You can secure the door from the inside for your safety. There has never been a problem in my home with thievery."

"My apology I didn't mean to accuse anyone of theft. Living and traveling alone, I have always had a key to my room or hotel suite. It will be fine. I'll join you at six."

"Rest well, Miss Miller."

She waited until Ms. Elsie left the landing before entering the room. It was large with several windows that allowed the sun to lighten the area. The larger window faced a garden and a cloth-covered reading bench was provided. A table with two chairs stood across the room near a smaller window. The usual porcelain water pitcher, washbowl, and two towels were on a corner stand next to the wardrobe. She removed the uncomfortable boots, kicking them across the floor. Then opened the trunk finding the sheer robe before stripping down to her undergarments for comfort. Morlanna opened the windows allowing a warm breeze to flow across the room, vanishing the memory of constant rain, as she brushed and braided her long hair.

As she looked out the window into the garden, Morlanna would always be thankful for parents who encouraged a love of reading. When the outside couldn't provide entertainment, the inside of a book would take her somewhere new. Thankfully, the library in Houston was located across the street from the hotel and kept her from going mad. The first visit was intense as she confronted the older librarian with a simple request.

The older woman raised her head and looked through the small-framed glasses at Morlanna. "I beg your pardon. What type of books are you requesting?"

"I don't believe I spoke in a foreign language, but I will repeat my request. I am interested in the section on books involving the occult. If you aren't familiar with its meaning, I'll make it simple; demons, devil worship, and witchcraft."

The woman cleared her throat. "No need for you to be insulting. I am not in the habit of having decent God-fearing young women ask for such abhorrent reading material."

"I feel it is important to know one's enemy through study, don't you?" Morlanna asked.

"I suggest you study the holy word of God if you wish to understand your enemy," she said. The woman stood and walked past Morlanna down a hallway, where she unlocked a door. "Please contact me as you leave, this door is to be locked when not in use."

"Thank you, now, if you would be so kind, to indicate where the smoking lounge is located."

"Shall I bring you a whiskey too?"

"If you have some available."

"The smoking room will be out the door and to your left," she said and whisked by Morlanna.

She may have gone too far asking for the whiskey. Over the years, her abruptness and rigid manner tended to upset men and women alike. A strong father figure and four older brothers were to blame for these accusations. Morlanna's mother even scorned him for their daughter's rough edges, but it kept men from taking advantage of her womanly virtues.

Morlanna glanced at the trunk and drug herself back, removing and separating the soiled clothes from the clean. She decided the empty wall next to the bed would be the perfect place to pin photographs, maps, and articles for immediate access over searching thru multiple stacks of information. She took a quick smoke break using the mint water in the atomizer to disguise the odor. The rules didn't say anything about smoking, but she knew Ms. Elsie would have a location for such habits outside the house.

The day waned into the evening, and she eased down the hallway toward the bathroom in her dressing robe. She stopped at the sound of voices echoing below.

"Do you think she will join us, Elsie?"

"Clara, the woman just arrived. We can't expect her acceptance of our beliefs immediately."

"I am excited to meet someone from California, do you think she knows Mrs. Winchester?"

Morlanna stifled a giggle at the last comment. She has stumbled into a group of believers. It would be interesting to see how quickly they included her in their group discussions of the occult. She hurried into the lavatory and then back to the room, choosing a relaxed outfit to make her appear approachable. She walked heavily down the stairs and delayed the entry for dramatic value. Six women immediately stood up as Morlanna entered the parlor, greeting her.

"Oh, I'm so sorry. I didn't mean to interrupt," she told them.

"Not at all, dear. We've been discussing the day's news, including your arrival," Elsie said.

Morlanna touched her breast. "I'm honored."

Elsie glanced toward the ladies. "Allow me to make introductions."

She listened closely, making mental notes and associations to remember them correctly. The ages varied from the mid-twenties to the late sixties. "It's a pleasure making your acquaintance."

"I don't know about anyone else, but I'm famished," Clara said.

"The dining room is set for us. Bernadette, would you help me in the kitchen?"

"Of course, Elsie."

"We have decided you should sit at the head of the table being our guest,"

Anne-Marie said.

"Shouldn't Ms. Elsie have the honor? She is the head of the house," Morlanna asked.

"I insist," Elsie stated, entering the room with a tray.

"You're very kind," she said, taking a seat. Each of the women seemed to have an assigned place arranged at the table. Ms. Elsie took a seat to her right, and Martine to her left.

"Estelle, would you please grace the table?" Elsie asked.

A frail woman stood holding her arms out. "We are blessed and thankful for our enlightenment."

"Estelle, you always have the right words for our gatherings," Anne-Marie said.

Morlanna was fascinated with the blessing and positive there would be much to learn from these women. They may have the information she needed to complete the research on the Bishop's Palace. She hoped it would not take the entire length of the stay for one of them to make an invitation. Their immediate questions were about her unusual name, life in California, and working in a man's world. Any concerns of being accepted by them dissolved by the end of their meal. They proceeded back into the parlor for warm brandy.

"If all the meals are like dinner, my skirts will need to be let out. It has been a lovely evening, but I'm quite tired and need to retire. It would be nice if I could see everyone again. Is this a possibility?"

Everyone smiled, glancing around the room from one to another. "We would be honored if you would join us once a week for conversation," Estelle told her.

"And more warm brandy," Clara said.

"It will be my pleasure unless my work or research conflicts," Morlanna explained.

"We may be helpful with your research," Bernadette said.

She smiled at them. "I look forward to your assistance, good night, ladies."

She left the room, slowly walking up the stairs hoping to hear their whispers. It seemed Ms. Elsie's was the perfect place for her, but the warning from Mr.

Guidry could mean it held another secret.

Parlor Conversation

As Morlanna left, the parlor came alive with whispers and excitement. Elsie raised her hand and motioned for them to lower their voices. Their conversation quietly began once the upstairs door closed.

"I like her," Martine spoke up immediately.

"How did we get so lucky?" Clara asked.

"It's providence," Estelle told them.

They all nodded in agreement.

"I suggest we not wait long before we approach her," Anne-Marie suggested.

"I'll ask about her visit and work over the coming week," Elsie said.

"It would be nice if one or two of us could drop by for afternoon tea," Bernadette said.

"We must not push her, allow events to come naturally," Estelle warned.

"Estelle, you are our strength," Clara said.

"We must keep her away from Cecile Guidry. She'll ruin everything," Bernadette said.

Elsie raised a hand over her mouth.

"What have you done?" Martine asked.

"She asked for a laundress, I suggested Cecile."

The women all began speaking at once.

Elsie raised her hand, settling the concerns of everyone. "It will be fine. I'm dropping her clothing at the store. She will not have any direct contact with Cecile."

"No, but she will have contact with Leotis," Bernadette said.

"We can hope she won't find anything he has to say important," Martine said.

"Do you know why she's here?" Anne-Marie asked.

"I cannot say for positive. I believe it involves research on the palace," Elsie said.

"Do you have any proof of that?" Estelle asked.

"Gossip coming from Guidry's store about a stranger asking the swamp folks about it. Old man Benoit told me he spoke with the man over a drink. It's my understanding this man came here to stop someone or something. He wasn't clear on the details, but it might involve Miss Miller and the palace," Elsie answered.

"It's a good thing she's staying with you, Elsie," Clara said.

"At least we can help if she's open-minded," Anne-Marie said.

"We may need Mama Delphine if this is true about the palace," Estelle announced.

"The priestess, why?" Bernadette asked.

"Powerful evil dwells within those walls. We all know it and have felt it. I suggest we ask for guidance tonight," Estelle said.

The clock began chiming. "Ladies, it's time," Elsie said and stood, leading everyone to the back of the house. They entered a familiar doorway into the basement, where the door was closed and locked behind them.

Chapter 10

Sunday, September 14th
  Morning

The next morning Morlanna woke to the sound of birds chirping outside the window. She turned over in the bed, slowly opening both eyes blinking as her lapel watch marked the time of day. She bolted from the bed and ran over to look outside, not believing it was eleven-thirty.

"No, it can't be."

The long delays with little sleep, two sniffers of warm brandy, and a soft-down mattress would be her excuse to Ms. Elsie for the late rising. She grabbed a robe and headed toward the lavatory for a relaxing bath. The events of the previous evening played out in her mind in the sweet smell of rose water.

She noticed that her room seemed to be the only one out of five occupied. This made the conversation yesterday about holding the room somewhat humorous. The choice of clothing for today would not be difficult as three items in the wardrobe remained unspoiled. The navy skirt and light blue blouse with a simple hair design would be appropriate for the informal setting in the house.

She could hear movement downstairs and prepared an apology, entering the parlor. "Ms. Elsie, I'm quite embarrassed having slept so late and missing services."

"She is in the garden," Leotis said.

Morlanna jumped, not expecting a male voice. "Oh, Mr. Guidry, you startled me."

"My apology. I understand you have laundry for my wife."

"Yes, yes, I do, please, give me a moment."

Elsie walked into the parlor. "Good day, Miss Miller. I hope I didn't disturb you this morning."

"Not at all. I must admit I'm confused at my late rising," Morlanna told her.

"No worry. Mr. Guidry agreed to pick up your things when I mentioned the need for laundry services at church."

"Ms. Elsie, would you have a basket for my items? I have a number of items, " she asked.

"Of course," she answered, disappearing for a moment.

Morlanna turned toward him. "I've been told your wife is a wonderful laundress. I'll be happy to pay whatever she asks as they are in dire shape."

"Here you are, dear." Elsie stepped between them, holding a basket.

She moved back, surprised at the intrusion between them. "I'll return in a moment."

"Mr. Guidry will be on the porch waiting for you."

Leotis turned, leaving the house.

Morlanna hurried upstairs, gathering everything except personal items. She would wash them in the lavatory. Ms. Elsie's rudeness seemed out of place and unnecessary for his kindness to personally pick up the clothes.

He opened the screen door allowing her outside, taking the basket. "These will be done by Thursday if that's acceptable."

"It will be fine. If more time is needed, please don't rush her. Mr. Guidry, I wish to apologize for Ms. Elsie's abruptness."

He shook his head. "It's her way, Miss. Have a nice day."

She watched him walk away and turned back toward the door when Ms. Elsie called her name.

"Miss Miller, I have tea and muffins, or would you like something else?"

"Meat and eggs if it's not too much to ask."

"Not at all, there is tea in the parlor."

"In a moment," she said, and couldn't understand why his wagon wasn't in front of the house. She walked to the road, discovering its location some distance away. A small woman waited in the wagon and faced away from the boarding house. There seems to be some discord between the Guidrys and Ms. Elsie.

The smell of bacon caused her stomach to rumble, retuning inside the house. She entered the parlor poured a cup of tea and proceeded into the dining room where two settings were waiting. Ms. Elsie appeared, carrying a tray of scrambled eggs, bacon, biscuits, and jam.

"Goodness, I didn't mean for you to bake fresh biscuits," Morlanna told her.

"I baked before church, and just warmed them up for us. Please, sit down and eat," she said.

As they took their seats, Ms. Elsie made the sign of the cross, praying silently. This could not be the same woman sitting to her right the previous night. Morlanna ate everything she placed on her plate, taking the last biscuit covering strawberry jam over it.

"I didn't think I could be hungry after last night's meal, but another wonderful meal. Thank you."

"My pleasure. I have always enjoyed cooking for others. More tea?"

She held up a hand. "I do have a question about Mr. Guidry."

Elsie poured a cup of tea for herself. "What do you wish to know?"

"Is there an issue between the two of you?"

She placed the teacup down and smiled. "We have some conflict in beliefs outside the church. I assure you it will not interfere with your stay."

Morlanna nodded and knew the conflict was over the weekly meetings held in the house. "One other question."

"Goodness, you are inquisitive today."

"I never know how individuals will react, but is there a place I can sit and enjoy a smoke?"

"Inquisitive and daring. Yes, there is a sitting area behind the house near the garden you may use. I would ask you not to smoke in my house," Elsie told her.

"I didn't see anything in the rules about the use of tobacco products but felt it proper to ask before using them. If you will excuse me, I'd like to go outside and familiarize myself with your home. I plan to work the rest of the day upstairs on my research."

"Clara and Bernadette will be coming later for afternoon tea. I hope you'll join us."

Morlanna smiled. "Lovely. Can I help clear the table?"

"No need. Go take your walk and enjoy the garden," she said and gathered the dishes from the table.

Morlanna stood and made her way back upstairs, locating her tin, matches, and notebook. She walked out the front door thinking the weather seemed more like summer than fall. She took a moment to enjoy a cigarette in the small floral sitting area before opening the notebook. The sight of a large amount of mint made her smile, making mental note to take several pieces upstairs. This simple plant could remove the smell of tobacco from her hands and breath.

Next week would be difficult being a stranger in town. The first thing necessary would be to make friends and refrain from asking too many questions. She would need to find the clerk's office for landowners in the area. The information she received through letters would need verifying with in-person interviews. She thought of Ms. Elsie's group and leaned back on the bench. It would take a bit of acting if she wished to be accepted. A non-believer would be shunned and not given any information if discovered.

Mr. Guidry's wife would be another individual she would like to have a conversation with as the woman definitely had no connection to anyone in the boarding house.

"Excuse me," a male voice said.

Morlanna raised her head, quickly dropping the cigarette and stepping on it. "May I help you?"

He smiled. "I'm attempting to locate the owner, Ms. Elsie. I have a reservation."

"I'm sure she is inside the house. I am Morlanna Miller," she said and stood to shake his hand.

The man bowed, took her hand, and kissed it. "Renaud Pierre Thibodeaux, it is my pleasure, Mademoiselle."

It had been a long time since anyone greeted her in such a manner. She found it enduring, though passé. "Renaud, you said?"

"Yes, please call me Ren."

She smiled, thinking Ms. Elsie could not possibly be aware her new boarder was a man. Morlanna could imagine the expression on the woman's face knowing he must have a written confirmation as she did after acquiring a reservation.

"Why don't you follow me? I'm sure she will be happy to have you as a guest."

They walked around to the front of the house as Clara and Bernadette arrived for afternoon tea. She found their expressions amusing as they seemed surprised to see the gentleman standing next to her.

"Morlanna, who is your friend?" Clara asked.

Ms. Elsie opened the screen door and walked outside before she could answer. She stopped at the sight of a bag sitting on the porch. "Young man, is this bag yours?"

Morlanna stepped forward, taking command of the situation. "Ms. Elsie, let me introduce Mr. Ren Thibodeaux, your new boarder. I've told him how nice it will be to have another guest in the house."

Elsie looked toward her friends. "This is quite a situation as I do not normally rent to men and women, at the same time."

"Ms. Elsie, it's 1890. Are we not civilized? I'm sure Mr. Thibodeaux has a written confirmation for his lodging. I will have no issue with his presence upstairs," Morlanna said.

"Elsie, you have always honored your word on boarders. It would be unwise to refuse," Bernadette said.

"It appears they are agreeable," Clara added.

"Of course, I will honor your reservation. A sign will be necessary on the lavatory door when in use, to assure your privacy."

She looked at Ren, who seemed to be amused by the entire conversation. "I see no issue, do you?"

"I will be happy to follow any rules, Ms. Miller," he said.

"Please come inside, sir, I need to collect some information from you," Elsie told him.

"Merci, Ms. Elsie. Mademoiselles," he said, picking up the case and entering the house.

Clara reached out, taking Morlanna's arm. "Where did you meet him?"

"He found me smoking in the garden."

Bernadette smiled. "Smoking, alone in the garden with a stranger. Be careful, or you'll have more rumors spreading through town than we do."

"Then it appears I am in good company," Morlanna said, smiling.

Bernadette glanced toward Clara. "I guess we should go inside, maybe he will join us for tea and cake."

"I just want to hear him speak again," Clara said.

"I'll join you in a moment. I left my notebook on the bench." She walked away, holding back the laughter. Mr. Thibodeaux would add intrigue inside the house and the weekly meetings. His black hair and beautiful brown eyes were mesmerizing and if she were guessing his age, probably a few years her senior. He seemed a man of means with the well-tailored clothing for his six-foot frame and shoes that were not worn or scuffed. His arrival, though not expected, might be a nice distraction. She found it strange he managed to walk up without her hearing him.

Clara hurried over as Morlanna entered the parlor. "We have some interesting information on Mr. Thibodeaux."

She looked around the room. "Are they in the kitchen?"

"No, Elsie took him upstairs to his room. He could be up there a while with her going over all the rules," Bernadette answered, grinning.

"There are two large rooms upstairs, yours and the first on the right as you reach the top landing. You will be running into him often," Clara said.

"I'm sure," Morlanna said.

"I heard him say he came to town on personal business for his family in New Orleans," Bernadette whispered.

"Did he give a length of time he would be staying?" Morlanna asked.

"He asked to keep the room for two weeks," Clara answered, smiling.

"Maybe you'll have another chance to meet in the garden," Bernadette said, glancing around Morlanna as footsteps descended the stairs.

The three of them turned to observe a smile on Elsie's face as they entered the parlor.

"Ladies, Ren has graciously accepted my invitation for tea."

"I have brought a taste of New Orleans," he said and produced a small tin of cookies. "I would be honored to share them."

Afternoon tea turned into the evening meal with Clara and Bernadette remaining until after dark.

"Clara, we must leave."

"May I accompany you both for safety?" he asked.

"Thank you, though it's not necessary. Our little town is safe, and we live close to one another." Clara answered.

"I'll see you to the door," Elsie told them.

"Will I see you, ladies, again?" he asked.

They smiled and nodded.

He turned toward Morlanna. "Should we help with the table?"

"It isn't necessary, Ren," Elsie said, entering the dining room.

Morlanna stood. "If you will excuse me, I have work waiting for me upstairs."

"Ms. Elsie, it has been a lovely evening, but I must retire after my journey."

"Breakfast will be at eight," she told them.

Ren followed her up the stairs. "Good night, Miss Miller."

She turned toward him. "Ne pas entrer dans leur web." Do not enter their web.

He nodded. "I will do my best to be careful."

Chapter 11

The Promise

Ren entered his room and began to unpack the suitcase still standing at the foot of his bed. The entire day had been an adventure, from secretly leaving his home to arriving at the boarding house. The atmosphere seemed almost carnival-like with his arrival. He found the ladies delightful but Morlanna most intriguing. She seemed to have a different perspective from the others, but that could be due to her living in a larger city. Ms. Elsie didn't think revealing information about her other boarder impolite and was happy to tell him all she knew.

He removed his clothing and personal items, taking out a package of letters. Ren remembered the day his mother gave them to him. She had been ill for months, and he knew it would not be long before God took her. She called him to her room one morning after his father left the house.

"Renaud, come and sit with me," she told him.

He sat down on the bed. "You look good, mother."

She took his hand and squeezed it. "Do not lie. It is a sin, and we both know I do not have much time left."

"Mother, please don't speak of your death."

"My son, we all die, but it is what we do on this earth to help others, charity and good works in the name of our Lord and holy mother that count."

"What is it you wish for me to do?"

She reached under her pillow and pulled a pack of letters out, handing them to him. "Our family has done a great injustice to the people in these letters. They have suffered too long. Your father will not listen to me and ignores my request and the pleas of the innocent."

"I do not understand."

His mother told the story of the bishop and what she believed to be their part in the evil cursing the parish.

"Renaud, promise me that you will try and help them."

"I don't know how."

"Read the letters, then go and find a way. The answer is there. Do not say anything to your father."

"Why?"

"He has been blinded by our wealth even though we give to the church. I feel his heart no longer feels pity."

"Mother." Ren could not believe her words.

"I will not rest peacefully until this evil is gone that has affected so many in that parish."

He believed his mother's soul could be suffering because he had not completed the task she gave him. Ren tried several times after she died to speak with his father about the bishop. He would ignore him or refuse to speak of monsters that did not exist. The suggestion their family contact the church and ask for their intervention met with Ren's father accusing him of blasphemy. He could see why his mother gave him this responsibility but remained divided between honoring her and his duty to the Thibodeaux legacy.

There would be some who would criticize a well-educated man for believing in such fables. He felt education made it possible for him to believe such a thing as the bishop could exist. If this evil existed, there would be a way to stop or destroy it.

He would not have much time before his father would begin to search for him or send others. Ren didn't know where to start his search, but it appeared the boarding house might be the center of information and town gossip. If he continued to be the proper gentleman, information could easily be gathered by simply listening.

Morlanna's company would be a nice distraction, and she seemed to be different from the women back home vying for his attention. They were only interested in his wealth, but this woman preferred intellect over compliments. A rare lady and one he would need to step lightly with, or she would dismiss him.

He undressed and washed his face before slipping into the bed. As he closed his eyes, a woman spoke.

"I am not at peace."

Ren sat up and looked around the room, his eyes filling with tears. "You will, mother. I promise you will."

Chapter 12

Thursday, September 18th

Morlanna opened the door, picking up a tray of biscuits, jam, and a porcelain teapot, closing the door behind her. She poured a cup of tea, thinking how nice it would be to have room service and be away from the group, allowing her to focus on new information. For the last two days, she requested meals be sent upstairs due to the lack of proper clothing. The day dress, skirt, and blouse were now unsavory in the humid climate and needed to be cleaned. Cecile sent word that some of the dresses were badly damaged and the repairs would delay their return. At this point, she may have to purchase clothing from Guidry's store or borrow something from Clara as they were close to the same size.

She opened the window, careful to not be seen in the sheer robe, and enjoyed the breeze. It was difficult to keep her promise and not smoke in the room, but she honored Ms. Elsie's request. Morlanna thought about Ren's first evening at the boarding house, and how he couldn't finish his meal with all the questions and chatter from the ladies. She didn't have a complete opinion of him other than his gentle manners. It might be too early in their association to ask questions about his family business.

Their trip into the land office together provided partial information. The location she needed no longer existed, but the cemetery location was available. According to the witness letters, the palace would be in the same proximity. The local citizens were friendly and willing to speak until asked about the Bishop's Palace. Any mention of it made them turn and quickly walk away.

She didn't mention the palace when in Ren's company to avoid unwanted inquiries from him.

They stopped in the general store, where Morlanna was surprised at the fully stocked shelves including an area of personal items for women. She purchased several milled soaps and, pleased that her undergarments no longer would be washed in lye at the boarding house.

She turned around at the light knock on her door. "Yes, who is it?"

"Miss Miller, some of your clothes have returned, including a package from Guidry's. I have placed everything on a chair outside your door."

"Thank you, Ms. Elsie. I'll collect them in a moment."

"Will you be joining us for dinner or take your meal upstairs again?"

She shook her head and knew the arrival of clothing meant there would be no reasonable excuse for not going downstairs this evening. "I'll be joining you for dinner."

"I'm setting the table for seven tonight," she said.

"You might ask Anne-Marie or Martine to join us," Morlanna suggested.

"I'll send word and see if they are available."

She waited for the steps to fade before opening the door to gather the clothes. The lavatory door at the end of the hallway opened. Morlanna watched as Ren stepped out with a towel around his waist and nothing else. She stared like a schoolgirl at his body, forgetting her undress.

"Forgive me. I didn't think anyone would be on the landing. I'm rather embarrassed," he said.

"Don't be," she said, smiling, and then gathered up the clothes. After closing the door, she leaned against it and waited for her heart to stop racing. Then her next thought was of how they would manage to have a polite conversation after this encounter would be challenging for both.

Morlanna composed herself and looked at the dresses, petticoats, and heavy dressing robe. The scent of lavender and roses clung to all the items making everything fresh and clean. The package held a boy's plaid shirt, pants, and items necessary for riding horseback. She would make arrangements for a horse to be delivered before dawn to the house and slip away before Ms. Elsie left for church. This first trip out would be to verify the palace existed.

The next and important visit would be when she entered the building to document the stories from the town. She would make sketches of the actual damage in her notebook to prove the legends false. The time had arrived when she must have a conversation with the ladies as they were withholding information from her. She grabbed the dressing robe and smoking tin, slipping barefoot down the stairs to the garden. The smell of the match burning and the first full inhale of tobacco was her favorite part of smoking.

"You're in danger," a female voice told her.

She stood up, dropping the cigarette. "Hello. Are you speaking to me?"

"There is nothing for you in the devil's house, leave now, or you will end up like your friend."

"What friend, who are you? Show yourself!"

"Miss Miller is someone bothering you?" Ren asked.

Morlanna turned around and stumbled back into a bush. He hurried over to help her up.

"You shouldn't sneak up on people."

"Who were you talking to?" he asked.

She pointed toward a stand of trees. "I think someone is out there."

"Wait here," Ren said and walked away to search the area.

She returned to the bench, waiting for him to come back.

"There is no one there," he told her.

"Well, I certainly didn't imagine it," she told him.

They heard the back door open and several voices speaking.

"Oh, Miss Miller," Clara said.

"We didn't mean to disturb you," Anne-Marie said, blushing.

"Miss Miller has received a threat," he said.

Clara ran to the back door. "Elsie, please come quickly we have a problem in the garden."

Morlanna closed her eyes and then glanced up at Ren. "Thanks."

The back door flew open, and a flurry of skirts hurried toward her location. "Miss Miller, are you harmed?" Elsie asked.

"No, just perplexed. Each time I come outside to enjoy my habit, there is an interruption."

"Who is threatening you?" Clara asked.

She tilted her head for a moment at the question. "Clara, if I knew, none of this would not be happening. I would have confronted the person."

"Male or female?" Elsie asked.

"The voice sounded female," Ren asked.

"What did she say?" Anne-Maire asked, sitting down.

Morlanna looked at everyone else standing in a protective stance around the bench. "The voice said I am in danger."

"Danger?" Elsie asked, stepping forward.

"Something about a house," Ren answered.

She realized he heard more of the conversation than she thought. Was he following her, and if so, why? "I'm sure this is a mistake of some type."

The three women looked at each other.

"What about your friend?" he asked.

"I have no idea. I'm confused like everyone else," Morlanna told them.

"Pardon my intrusion," a deep male voice said.

Ren looked up. "Father?"

Morlanna shook her head and wondered why she ever thought the garden would be a safe place.

Ren turned to the women. "Ladies, my father, Jean-Philippe."

He bowed. "I apologize for my unexpected arrival. Ms. Elsie, I understand you are the proprietor of this boarding house. I hope you might have a room available for me."

Morlanna watched as Elsie began to smile.

"Why of course, unfortunately, Miss Miller and your son have the larger rooms, but I promise you will be comfortable."

"It will be an honor to stay in your home," he said.

"Miss Miller, please excuse me. I should see to Ren's father, Anne-Marie, or Clara will stay with you," Elsie said.

Both the women seemed perturbed at the suggestion.

"I will be fine and do not need a chaperone," Morlanna stated.

"Are you sure?" Clara asked.

"Please go, I'd like to try and smoke one complete cigarette," she said, watching everyone hurry away. Morlanna lit another cigarette and headed to the area, she felt the voice originated. She discovered a small space in the middle of three trees where someone could stand unobserved and view the entire garden area.

The only sign anyone had been in the area were several strands of bells hanging in the trees above her. The glint of something circular made her blink. She searched the ground for a broken limb to reach the object. It finally fell to the ground after several attempts to reach it. She took a moment to inspect the unfamiliar design on the copper circle, then stepped back to view the location. Ren could have easily reached the limbs above her. The warning and his presence coinciding with her arrival left several unanswered questions in her mind.

Morlanna returned inside, slipping upstairs unseen and into the lavatory. She placed the occupied sign outside and filled the tub, allowing the afternoon events to float away in the steam. The sweet smell of rose and steamy water made her ignore the sounds outside the lavatory. The water hadn't begun to cool when a light knock on the door indicated her bath was over.

"Yes, Ms. Elsie."

"I hate bothering you, dear, but Jean-Philippe would like to freshen up before dinner."

She pulled the stopper from the drain with a toe. "I'm stepping out now."

"I'll inform him. He is such a lovely man and has brought champagne from New Orleans," she announced.

Not bothering to dry completely, she opened the door dressed in her robe and towel around her head. Ms. Elsie moved away as the steam poured out of the lavatory. "It sounds like a splendid evening."

She stepped forward and smiled. "I've sent word to the rest of our little group to come tonight."

Morlanna glanced toward the stairs as heavy footsteps began ascending. "I can't wait. If you don't mind, I prefer Mr. Thibodeaux and his son, not find me in a robe again. Once in the garden was enough."

"Of course, dear, I imagine it was quite embarrassing for you," she said, then walked away, leaving Morlanna in the lavatory doorway.

As the time approached for dinner, she looked in the wardrobe mirror at her hair and dress for this evening, spraying a small amount of perfume on both wrists. Morlanna didn't wish to join the activities tonight after the conversation with Ms. Elsie in the lavatory. The decision to be a part of the noise instead of hearing it all night echoing in her room seemed to be the better choice. The charm discovered in the tree bothered her knowing Ren could have placed it there though she had no proof. The cigarette tin and matches were slipped in the pocket of her dress, hoping for at least one uninterrupted private moment this evening. Ren and his father stood on the landing and turned as she exited the room.

"Mademoiselle Miller may I properly introduce to my father, Jean-Phillipe Thibodeaux."

She held out her hand.

He took her hand and placed his hand lightly on top. "Charmé et honoré." Charmed and honored.

"As I am, sir," she responded.

Jean-Phillipe turned to his son and nodded.

"We should go. I'm sure the ladies are anxious to meet you," she said.

"After you Miss Miller," Ren said.

"I appreciate your propriety Ren, but please, call me Morlanna as I suggested the first day we met."

"As you wish, Morlanna," Ren said.

The evening was worse than the day Ren arrived. She preferred to have a conversation with men over the prattle of women. The evening conversations around the dinner table with her brothers were filled with challenges. In the beginning, she never seem to best them, until her father encouraged deeper reading from their library. Morlanna became adept at holding a serious conversation among men.

Jean-Philippe, thank you for bringing such excellent champagne, it made a nice aperitif," Elsie told him.

"I have never tasted a better duck and the sauce, Magnifique," Jean-Phillipe said.

Elsie blushed. "A family recipe of honey and mint."

"Superb, none better in New Orleans," he continued complimenting her.

Stories and never-ending inquires graced the table before everyone retired to the parlor for dessert and brandy. Morlanna took this time to slip out into the garden, and before a match could be struck, she heard footsteps.

"I hope you don't mind me joining you, I needed a break," Ren said.

"Your father might have been happier sleeping at the livery," she said, laughing.

"He enjoys the company of women, all women."

"I suspect your mother is not pleased," she said and noticed him look away.

"My mother passed away several years ago."

"I'm sorry."

"What is in the trees?" he asked, pointing behind her.

She stood up and ran toward the lights flickering in the trees.

"Morlanna wait!"

Just before she reached the trees, the lights disappeared. The sight of smoke filling the area made her stop, allowing Ren to catch up.

"You must be cautious of the dangers here. There are many creatures which can cause death if bitten."

She held up a hand and pointed to the trees taking a deep breath. "Incense?"

He sniffed the air shaking his head. "Sandalwood."

She could hear the change in the tone of his voice. "Is that a problem?"

"Sandalwood is used in Voodoo practices."

"Voodoo?"

"A powerful religion practiced in many areas of Louisiana. They have priests and priestesses who use talismans and incense for many reasons."

"Why is sandalwood burned?" she asked and thought of the charm.

"It's a sacred wood used to purify or sanctify an area. We should leave, until we know why someone is placing spells," he said and took her hand.

She pulled away, looking at him. "Spells?"

"Yes, there is no other purpose for its use," he told her.

"Aren't you the least curious about who was here tonight? I certainly am."

He kept glancing from one direction to another. "If this person wanted you to see them, they would have remained to answer your questions."

"Ren, Miss Miller," Jean-Phillipe called.

She looked back toward the trees. "You don't feel we should go any further, do you?"

"Ren!"

"No, please come," he said, holding out his hand to her. "Please."

This action went against everything she believed in as a reporter. Morlanna ran towards a story, never away from one. "Alright, but I will not be chased away by smoke and lights next time."

They walked back to where Jean-Phillipe stood. "Is there a problem?"

Ren smiled and squeezed her hand. "We needed some air."

Jean-Philippe smiled. "Come, the ladies are asking for you. They have more questions."

"I'm sure they do," she told him.

Chapter 13

Sunday, September 21st
  Morning

She checked the night sky from the window and finished buttoning the plaid shirt. Morlanna thought about the past few days since Jean-Phillipe's arrival. The boarding house had been abuzz with landowners from the area vying daily in hopes of selling their land for a decent profit. Ms. Elsie's group of ladies were fascinated with the men from New Orleans and were always present for afternoon tea or evening brandy. The constant interruptions were not the environment needed to complete her work.

She opened the door, hoping the noise would go unnoticed as it wasn't unusual for anyone to move about for personal reasons this early. Morlanna carried a pair of boots down the stairs, avoiding the squeaky steps to prevent anyone from seeing her in men's apparel. The provisions hidden in the garden were gathered and placed on the horse left by the livery. She mounted and headed away from the boarding house as the eastern sky began to lighten.

The Observer

Jean-Philippe watched as Morlanna rode away from the house before dawn from his window. He turned at the light knock on his door.
  "Come."
  The door opened, and he motioned for his son to join him at the window.
  "You're up early, father."

"And you?"

"I have something which needs my attention and didn't wish to wake Morlanna or Ms. Elsie."

He pointed out the window. "You see the rider in the distance?"

"The boy."

Jean-Philippe shook his head no. "Miss Miller is out for an early ride."

Ren shook his head and walked away.

"Is there a problem I should know about?" Jean-Philippe asked.

Ren frowned. "The other night when you were looking for us."

He smiled. "A stolen kiss? No harm."

"No. We were talking in the garden and lights appeared in the trees. She ran toward the trees before I could warn her of the dangers."

"The two of you seemed fine," Jean-Philippe told him.

"Someone was burning sandalwood."

Jean-Philippe crossed himself. "Who is casting spells? Have you spoken with your aunt?"

"No, but I am sure she knows we are here."

"Ren, what have you been drawn into?"

"Unsure."

A small bell rang out at the bottom of the stairs.

"It seems we are not the only ones up early," Jean-Philippe said.

"What do we tell her about Morlanna?"

Jean-Philippe shook his head. "Say nothing."

"I must, or Ms. Elsie will be knocking on her door. I'll say she asked not to be disturbed."

"You should not become involved in Miss Miller's problems."

"I believe her problems are our problems."

"Jean-Philippe–?" called Elsie.

"Yes, Ms. Elsie."

"There is tea on the dining table."

"Merci, we will be down shortly."

"Will you be escorting the ladies to church?" Ren asked.

"Yes. This unnecessary trip to bring you home became a successful opportunity to purchase land. I should express appreciation to God for His blessings, and you?"

"No. I have business in the woods."

"I'll make excuses at breakfast for your absence at church. I will ask that you protect yourself. Now, we must go downstairs."

The Search

An hour after breakfast, Ren stood watching his father leave the house with Ms. Elsie and two of the ladies. He returned upstairs and stood outside Morlanna's room.

"I'm sorry," he said, closing his eyes in silent apology.

Ren reached for the knob, turned it, and entered her room. Over the next few minutes, he walked around the room, stopping in front of the wall which held maps and newspaper stories on the Bishop's Palace. He tried to be careful and not to disturb her papers.

He picked up the leather journal, scanned through the entries, and stopped when she detailed the plan to enter the Bishop's Palace. Morlanna's bravery and determination would be her undoing one day. As he replaced the journal, the sun glinted off an item on the table. Fear overtook him at the recognition of the object.

"Loa Eshu," he said and backed away, never taking his eyes off the talisman. Ren began repeating words of protection as he left the room.

The front door opened, making him jump and turn around as footsteps moved up the stairs. Ren could not believe how quickly the time had passed since entering Morlanna's room.

Jean-Philippe reached the landing. "What has happened? You look as though you have seen the devil."

Ren glanced toward Morlanna's room. "Loa Eshu. She has his talisman."

He held a finger on his lips and pulled Ren away from the stairs toward his room. "Are you positive?"

"Yes."

Jean-Philippe opened the door, motioning for Ren to follow him. "I am leaving in two days, and you will go with me."

"I cannot."

"You will!"

Ren could not believe his father intended to walk away. "How did you find me?"

"The servants have been loyal to our family long before you were born. They notified me when I returned from the city."

"Why the lie about purchasing land? We do not need more property," Ren asked.

"Would you prefer for these women to know you are a runaway child searching for monsters? You must stop this ridiculous obsession that we owe these people anything."

"That's not what mother believed. I've read the letters from these people begging for our help to stop this evil. If our ancestor had not given the land, we would not be responsible for the trouble hanging over the parish," Ren told him.

"I told your mother to burn them."

"She didn't and gave them to me before her death. I promised to try…"

He held up a hand at Ren. "Enough! We are not responsible for the past. You are my son and will do as I ask. Speak no more of this to me or anyone in the house."

"Mother is not at rest and will not leave purgatory until we do what is right."

"How dare you suggest such a horrible thing to me."

"Jean-Philippe, will Ren be joining us?" Elsie's voice called out from the bottom of the stairs.

Ren shook his head no.

"Yes, he will."

"Father," Ren whispered angrily.

He held up a hand. "I've been informed Miss Miller left the house after we went to church. She will return later today."

"Oh, I hope it isn't anything serious. Did she say anything before leaving?" Elsie asked.

"No," Ren answered.

"Very well, I'll leave a plate for her tonight in the kitchen," she told them.

"I'm sure she will be grateful for your generosity," Jean-Philippe said.

They listened as her footsteps faded.

"Why did you lie?" Ren asked.

"Do you wish to explain her absence before the sun rose?"

Ren shook his head no.

"Nor do I. This discussion is over, do you understand, over? Go wash up and place a jacket on. I'll meet you in the parlor."

Ren watched his father descend the staircase. He loved him, but this was not the answer, running away and leaving everyone in danger. They should not ignore or deny their family's past. When the priest died, their ancestor should have requested the land be returned. His father taught him as a child to honor his word when given, but the bishop's words held no honor to the people or to God.

As the day progressed from afternoon into evening, he excused himself and walked out into the trees once more. Nothing except several strings of bells hung from several branches. He remained outside until the lights of the boarding house were no longer burning, leaving him in the darkness. His concern for Morlanna's safety intensified as the hours passed.

Shortly after midnight, he heard footsteps on the porch. "Did you have a nice day?"

She pulled the derringer backing up against the door. "Christ! I almost shot you."

It took a strong woman to stand and point a gun in the face of any man. "I can see now I shouldn't have been concerned when you left this morning."

She replaced the derringer in her pocket. "I went to search for an old cemetery, but the information from the land office kept me lost most of the day."

"Did you find what you were searching for?"

"No. If you don't mind, I would like to go inside to avoid any confrontation with your father or Ms. Elsie. An explanation of returning in men's clothing and unchaperoned is not a conversation I wish to have right now."

"I doubt you care what anyone thinks, Morlanna Miller. I am happy you have returned safely."

"Good night, Ren," she said and quietly moved into the house.

He nodded and left the porch walking back into the garden. The smell of sandalwood hung low in the air, and the lights in the trees had returned. Ren took a silver medallion of St. Michael from beneath his shirt, kissed it, and then began to pray. He hoped this action would protect him and those inside the house.

Chapter 14

Tuesday, September 23rd

Morlanna stood outside, joining the rest of her acquaintances in bidding farewell to Jean-Philippe and Ren. There were tears mixed with continuous promises to visit his home in New Orleans as a group. Ms. Elsie presented a large basket of baked items for their short trip home by train. She had never seen such sadness expressed except at funerals and chose to remain on the porch rather than directly participate. This position allowed her a full view of the scene taking place.

Mr. Guidry arrived early to transport the men to the train station, but the lengthy farewells were making the horses irritable.

Jean-Philippe took this as his cue. "Mademoiselles, it is time. We must regretfully depart. You have filled our lives with such joy these few days.

Ren glanced toward the porch and walked through the women as his father began kissing hands and receiving mementos from the ladies.

Morlanna stifled a laugh as Ren reached her location. "He's quite the gentleman. Did he happen to study the theatre arts?"

Ren sighed. "I find all of this distasteful," he said, slowly smiling. "He does enjoy charming the ladies."

"And you?"

"It is not my way and never shall be. I would like your permission to exchange correspondence in the future?"

"You are a strange individual," she answered, sliding a piece of paper from the cuff of her sleeve into his hand.

He raised her hand to his lips. "Au revoir, until we meet again."

She nodded as he walked away and watched as the women followed both men to the wagon standing in the road waving. She entered the house, going upstairs to check the rest of her dresses Mr. Guidry returned this morning. He refused to take any additional payment for his wife's work. A skillful seamstress, even in a large city is difficult to find, and Morlanna felt fortunate to be Cecile's client. As she hung the dresses in the wardrobe, a book fell on the floor, scattering money at her feet.

Morlanna recognized the book immediately as she'd seen Wilson Derby use it many times at work. She picked up the journal and the money counting a total of five hundred dollars. As she began reading his recent entries, Morlanna slammed the book shut.

"Ludsworth, you are a worthless human being, but I didn't expect you to conspire against me."

Ludsworth's disdain for her knew no boundaries, but to send clueless Wilson out to do his dirty work, was laughable. She wondered if he might still be in the area? Why would he leave so much money? She assumed it belonged to him, and why hadn't anyone in town mentioned another stranger? The voice in the trees suggested something unfortunate happened to her friend. It had to be Wilson.

"Morlanna!"

She didn't want or need company at this moment but knew Anne-Marie would come upstairs if the call went unanswered. "I'm putting away my dresses."

"Elsie has opened a bottle of Jean-Philippe's wine he left for us. Everyone is so excited about planning our trip. We have some questions for you. I'm hoping you will change your mind and join us."

"I'll be honored assisting in preparations for such a fun adventure and pleased you've asked for my opinion. I'll be down in a moment."

"Hurry."

Morlanna needed to work, but with all the excitement in the house, it would not be possible today. She hoped everyone would drink, talk and leave. If not, she would be smoking in the garden by lantern light after dark.

Fortunately, several ladies had duties at home and left early. She found it interesting Martine and Bernadette were married, yet they came and went without issue from their husbands. She felt it must be cultural for the area. In polite society, married women were not seen out socially unless accompanied by a spouse. Morlanna assisted Ms. Elsie in cleaning the parlor and removing the dishes and glasses into the kitchen.

"Miss Miller, would you mind if we forgo dinner tonight?"

"Not at all. I'll be happy attending to myself."

"Thank you, I'm finding myself quite melancholy and would prefer being alone," she said.

"I understand. Jean-Philippe is charismatic, don't you agree?" she asked.

"He lightened every corner of this old house. I find him fascinating," Elsie told her.

"Hopefully, this excursion to New Orleans will lift your spirits again."

Elsie nodded. "Yes, I believe it will."

The effect this one man had over these women bewildered Morlanna. The comment Ren made to her might be sincere, indicating Jean-Philippe truly enjoyed the company of women, showing his feelings through words and actions. The ladies seemed to be deprived of such compliments and she needed to be considerate of that yearning.

She decided to sit on the front porch to read Wilson's notebook and didn't care if the entire town saw her smoking in the open. The garden no longer seemed welcoming with the discovery of the charm and lights. Morlanna read through several pages and laughed out loud at the description of his accommodations on the Guidry property. Wilson's last entry detailed his plan to destroy the palace just two days before her arrival. She discovered a folded page with a map and directions to the Bishop's Palace. Leotis Guidry's involvement seemed due to him being the center of everything in town. Ludsworth always knew who he could sway with money. Either Cecile or Leotis had placed the book and money in her dresses.

The sound of a wagon stopping made her stand up as a man walked toward the house. "Mr. Guidry."

He nodded, removing his hat. "I thought you might want some information about the book," he said and pointed toward her hand.

"Would you like to come inside?"

He shook his head no. "Please call me Leotis."

She smiled. "If you wish."

"If you could stop by the store tomorrow around ten, I will explain everything to you."

"I'll be there," she answered.

He turned, walking away from her.

"Leotis, what about the money?"

He looked over his shoulder. "Keep it, or give it away. I do not want it."

Chapter 15

Wednesday, October 1st

A cool breeze greeted Morlanna as she left the house heading toward town. The forty-five-minute walk gave her time for contemplation on the upcoming conversation. After Leotis's visit yesterday, she spent the rest of the evening reading through the notebook closely. The multiple misspelled words made her wonder how Wilson managed to stay employed at the newspaper. His entire trip had one purpose, to see her dismissed and disgraced as a reporter.

The sight of numerous wagons in front of Guidry's store and people milling around inside made her decide to walk another twenty minutes to the livery stable. She made arrangements for this Friday night's excursion before heading back to the store. Her initial trip failed due to false information, but now she had a real map.

It appeared Wednesday was the day for purchasing goods before the weekend. Her interaction with several ladies in town relieved fears the stories of lights, and sandalwood remained inside the boarding house. The unusual amount of customers in the store could mean their meeting might be canceled or delayed.

"Miss Miller," Leotis said.

She turned. "Yes."

"I have your order in the back. Please follow me," he said and moved around the counter, opening a small curtain.

"Thank you," she said, entering, unsure why he ushered her out of the main room. Daylight filled the back area, and the smell of coffee made her smile.

"Hello."

A small woman stepped around the corner. "Please come join me in a cup of café."

"Cecile?"

"Yes."

Morlanna entered an area containing extra supplies, and a small table stood with three chairs. She took a seat as Cecile prepared two cups of coffee for them, offering milk and sugar from a small silver tray on the table.

"I hope you like strong café it's the chicory we add," Cecile explained.

She took the cup and drank the black liquid smiling. "I have missed drinking coffee, Ms. Elsie only serves tea."

Cecile smiled. "Were you pleased with the dresses?"

"Oh yes. Did I pay you enough?"

She nodded. "Too much."

"Not at all. I've not seen such skill as yours even in San Francisco."

"You are too kind," Cecile said.

She took another sip of the coffee. "Did you place the notebook in my dress?"

"No, my husband. We felt you needed to know about Mr. Derby."

They looked up as Leotis walked into the room. "It's a busy morning. Miss Miller, can you wait a little longer? I usually close the store for lunch. Cecile has made gumbo, will you join us?"

She nodded. "I'd be honored to share a meal with you. Please, attend to your customers while we become acquainted."

He smiled and nodded at the women before leaving.

"You have a good husband. It seems he enjoys helping people."

Cecile remained silent for a moment. "He is a good man, and I pray to the holy mother every day in thanks for being so blessed. We made a terrible mistake helping Mr. Derby, and I worry that we have brought trouble into our home."

Morlanna didn't understand and hoped Leotis could explain Cecile's concerns. She followed her outside where a large pot hung over a small fire behind the store.

The smell of the food made her stomach grumble. "I must be in heaven."

"Have you eaten gumbo before?" Cecile asked.

"Not in many years."

She smiled. "Leotis says mine is the best in our parish."

"There is none better," he said, walking over and kissing her head. "We should eat first, then speak."

"Agreed."

Cecile filled three bowls with bread and gumbo before they walked back into the store.

"Wine, Miss Miller?" Leotis asked.

"Yes, thank you."

"My wife makes her gumbo spicy," he said.

"Sounds like my grandmother."

Leotis and Cecile looked at each other. "Are you Cajun?" he asked.

Morlanna took a bite of food, enjoying every flavor exploding in her mouth. She nodded, accepting the glass of wine, and cleared her palate. "French, Cajun, and Irish," she said, pointing at her red hair.

"Are you from the bayou?" Cecile asked.

"No. I was raised and educated in California. My grandparents lived south of Lafayette for years. They eventually came to live with us until their passing."

"Bless them," Cecile said, crossing herself.

She finished her food and picked up the glass of wine. "Thank you, Cecile, for a wonderful meal."

"My pleasure, may I get you more?" Cecile asked.

"No, but I would like to ask about the notebook and money," she told them.

Leotis finished his meal, refilling his glass. "Cecile, are you going to stay for this conversation?"

She shook her head no. "Excuse me, I do not feel comfortable speaking about Mr. Derby or the palace. It has been nice to meet you. Guard your soul," Cecile said and left, taking the dishes with her.

"You will have to excuse my wife. She is sometimes conflicted between religion and the beliefs of our people. What do you wish to know?"

Morlanna nodded. "Who contacted you from the newspaper?"

"Mr. Ludsworth sent a telegram inquiring to the lodgings in town. I informed him the boarding house should be the most respectable and a center of gossip. The next telegram said Wilson would be lodged away from the town in an uncomfortable manner with no running water or inside toilet. He sent a large sum of money for my trouble. Wilson should never have been sent here, too soft."

She began laughing. "I agree. Who drew the map?"

Leotis dropped his head. "I drew it for him. He talked with people in the swamp, asking questions like you. I'm sure you have realized by now that the location of the Bishop's Palace is not something anyone will speak of or admit to knowing directions. Two days before you arrived, he left everything at my farm and has not returned."

"His notes indicated he planned to destroy the palace."

Leotis shook his head. "It stands, and neither time nor storms have not damaged or changed it. If the creatures in the swamp did not kill Wilson, the bishop took him."

"You believe the palace is malevolent."

Leotis took a drink of his wine. "I have a question. Did your grandmother ever tell you stories about the swamps or bayous?"

Morlanna smiled. "She tried. My father would not allow them in his presence, so they became my bedtime stories. They were very interesting, but when he discovered what she was really doing the stories stopped."

"You missed an important part of your history."

"Why did you invite me here today?" she asked.

"I want to ask you not to follow in Wilson's footsteps."

"Leotis, It is difficult for me to understand the beliefs of the swamp, but I am here to write a story. I cannot return to San Francisco empty-handed without knowing where the truth lies. Wilson Derby's entire life revolved around money, which is extremely odd he left it. The unfortunate reality is he probably drank too much and fell into the bayou drowning, or a rich woman procured his services. I cannot believe a mythical demon bishop lured him to his death."

73

"Better you leave here alive than end up like him. I have done what Cecile asked of me. I beg you, please, stay away from the devil's house or you will lose your soul."

"I appreciate your concern, truly, but I came for a story, it's my job. Thank you again for the wine and meal."

He nodded.

She stood up and left out the back door of the store with more information than expected. With Wilson's notebook in her possession, she would force Ludsworth to publish the story in multiple editions. As she walked toward the boarding house, Morlanna knew one or more of the women had information concerning the palace. They all seemed to be guarding a secret, but whose?"

Chapter 16

Confessions

Morlanna's earlier conversation with the Guidrys' gave added inspiration for the meeting tonight. The sound of voices filling the boarding house seems to have helped Ms. Elsie's melancholy subside. She picked up the notebook and charm, placing them in a pocket before going downstairs. Her entry went unnoticed as everyone was hovering over Anne-Marie in the parlor.

Clara glanced up and noticed Morlanna. She ran over, grabbing both of her hands. "Have you heard the news?"

"No, though it appears interesting," she said.

"Ladies, ladies, I just received the telegram shortly before you arrived. I haven't had time to inform Miss Miller," Elsie said.

"Jean-Philippe has asked we change our plans and join him in New Orleans for the holidays," Anne Maire said.

"Why the sudden change?" Morlanna asked.

"He misses our spirit," Elsie answered with a huge smile across her face.

"He believes our presence will brighten his home with holiday cheer," Bernadette added.

"Please say you will change your mind and join us. It will be such a grand affair, plus we have all seen how Ren acts when he is around you," Clara told her.

Morlanna didn't answer and took a moment listening as everyone twittered about the room. She glanced toward Martine and Bernadette who were even more excited than the others.

"Is everyone going?" she asked them.

"Yes," Anne-Marie answered.

"His home must be quite large as he has welcomed all of us, including family members," Estelle answered.

"Goodness, such an offer is quite generous," she said.

"We have so much to discuss," Elsie told them.

"Yes, we do. I have information to share this evening," she told them.

"It sounds like a late night for all of us," Bernadette said.

"I suggest we get started," Martine suggested.

"There's wine on the table. I'll be out with our meal in a few moments," Elsie said, taking the telegram from Anne-Marie and placing it in her pocket.

Jean-Philippe's telegram set off a flurry of anticipation regarding a New Orleans holiday. The invitation included the ladies and immediate family, all expenses paid by their host. The reasons for the change of dates seemed odd to her, almost patronizing in her opinion. She could see how a fully paid holiday would be tempting living in a small town. Their dinner conversation was a continuation of travel plans. They were all interested in the size of his house.

"He must have a house full of servants," Clara said.

"Of course. You do not invite guests expecting them to cook and clean," Anne-Marie told her.

"Shall we adjourn?" Elsie asked.

"I'd like for everyone to remain at the table for a little longer if you're agreeable," Morlanna told them.

"We can take our brandy in here," Estelle suggested.

Martine brought glasses and brandy from the parlor while Clara helped Elsie remove the dishes from the table.

"I have information for all of you and some questions," she told them, then stood watching as the ladies began looking at one another.

"Morlanna, you sound cross, have we upset you?" Anne-Marie asked.

She smiled. "Oh, no Anne-Marie, I didn't mean to sound agitated. I've felt nothing except warmth and acceptance from everyone at this table. It's time for a full explanation of my visit. I am a reporter from a newspaper in San

Francisco writing a story on the legend of the Bishop's Palace. The reading public is interested in the occult, and the stories of all the disappearances are intriguing."

The table became very quiet as the women looked from one to another.

"It isn't a legend," Martine said.

"The disappearances happened," Clara said.

These admissions were more than she expected, hopefully, they would continue to talk. "Have any of you seen a stranger in the area several weeks before my arrival?"

"I heard a man is staying out at the Guidrys'. He's been asking questions about the palace," Elsie said.

Morlanna reached in her pocket, laying the notebook on the table. She opened it, spreading the money across the table. The women gasped at the large amount in front of them. "A man named Wilson Derby was sent ahead of me to discredit my story by destroying the palace.

"Who is Wilson Derby?" Anne-Maire asked.

"He is another reporter from the same newspaper." Morlanna watched the women realizing they had not met Wilson. "He has disappeared."

"Did he enter the Bishop's Palace?" Estelle asked.

"I'm not sure, but according to the last entry, he intended to burn it down," she told them

The women began talking among themselves.

"Ladies. I need the truth, every detail you can tell me about the palace."

Estelle rose from her chair. "This is not something which concerns you."

She reached in her pocket again and pulled out the charm, throwing it across the table to Estelle. "You might want to reconsider your comment once you look at the amulet."

Estelle leaned over the table immediately recognizing the design. "Loa Eshu."

"Sit down Estelle, please," Elsie said.

"You must understand, we were excited about having a reporter from San Francisco visit our little town," Bernadette said.

"You all knew?" Morlanna asked.

77

Everyone at the table nodded.

"And you didn't say anything, why?" she asked.

"We believed you would inform us when you were ready," Clara answered.

"We didn't think much about the man staying with Leotis until you arrived with similar interests in the palace," Martine added.

"I'm aware you ladies are involved in occult practices," Morlanna told them.

"It's nothing bad," Clara said quickly.

"I bought a spirit board, and we've used it a few times. We were hoping you might join us one evening," Anne-Marie said.

"We all believed you would do your research, talk with a few people, and leave," Estelle said.

"The item in your hand makes leaving impossible, I need answers," she told them.

Elsie held out her hand. "Let me see it, Estelle." She took the charm staring at the design. "Where did you find this?"

"I discovered it hanging in the trees behind the garden."

"You found a talisman on my property?" Elsie asked.

She nodded. "The night Ren's father arrived."

Clare smiled. "We notice Ren left after you did."

"He joined me outside, and while we were speaking, noticed lights in the trees. I ran toward them, but they disappeared, leaving the scent of sandalwood filling the area. The next day I found the charm where the lights had been."

Bernadette gasped. "Someone is casting spells."

"It must be Mama Delphine," Estelle said.

"Why is she casting spells? If there is a problem, she should be approaching me instead of hiding in trees on my property," Elsie said.

"I'd like the opportunity to speak with her," Morlanna said.

"I'm not sure a meeting is possible," Estelle said.

"I prefer a proper introduction. A request coming from this group might influence her decision," Morlanna told them.

Elsie looked around the table at the women nodding. "Estelle, see if you can set up a meeting here at the house."

"She isn't always easy to find, but I'll try. There's a reason she is casting spells and leaving charms," Estelle said.

"If she doesn't feel comfortable in the house, I'll bring Miss Miller any place she wishes," Elsie said.

"I will need some time to look for her," Estelle stated.

"Thank you. Now, who can tell me the complete story of the Bishop's Palace?" Morlanna asked.

Estelle stood up. "If you will excuse me, I'd prefer not to be part of the next conversation."

"Ladies the information Miss Miller is asking about is not a group discussion. I'm sure all of you will understand," Elsie said.

Morlanna watched as everyone at the table rose, took their cloaks, and left the house.

Elsie stood up, holding the charm. "Bring your brandy, Miss Miller."

She felt a sudden chill as if a north wind blew across her face and arms. "Is there a window open?"

Elsie ignored the question, lighting the small stove in the corner of the parlor. "Please sit down. I have the information you are requesting."

Morlanna sipped her brandy, anxious to see if this woman would spin a tale to satisfy a big city reporter's curiosity.

"Is your information from a reliable source or small-town gossip?"

Elsie frowned. "Young lady, your impertinence is not needed. What I have to say is extremely personal and I ask you to be respectful of it."

She immediately regretted the earlier comment. Ms. Elsie had been nothing but kind and felt this information was important. The thought of needing a notebook and pen faded as the opportunity to leave had passed.

"My apologizes, please tell me about the palace."

Elsie took a sip of the brandy leaning back into the chair. "In 1815 the parish priest received a gift of land for a home and small garden. In exchange for this gift, the man donating the property asked the priest to make a daily trip to the cemetery and pray for the dead. A simple request the priest gladly agreed to for such a generous gift. Two years later the parish flourished, farms and families grew, and a new church was built. The priest sent a request

79

asking the bishop to come and bless the new church, but before the bishop could arrive the priest suddenly died."

Morlanna could see the woman beginning to shake.

"After the priest's burial, a group of men approached the bishop asking him to stay until another priest could be sent. The bishop understood the needs of the parish but respectfully declined the offer. He informed the delegation it could be years before another priest might be sent. Later the same day, two men from the group requested a private meeting. If the bishop would remain in the town, they promised him a wealth of gold, silver, and jewels. His duties would be to continue the spiritual care of the people in the parish and pray daily for the dead in the cemetery."

"Where did this treasure come from?"

She held up a hand. "The bishop asked for proof of such wealth from the men. They presented a small container filled with gold and silver coins to him, swearing they would give him more if he remained. Not only did he agree, but insisted the parish build a home honoring his standing as a representative of the holy church. Over the next two years, the men of the town built the bishop a home of great magnitude. They ignored their farms, causing the fields to wither, crops and cattle died, leaving the parish in a dire situation. The bishop continued to demand the grand home be finished at any cost."

"Did the men continue bringing him gold?"

She nodded. "Gold was given to him as promised, and he reveled in the riches refusing to give it to the church or needy in the parish. He failed to keep the simple request of prayers for the dead. His sermons became less of God's love and more of giving all one has to him. The bishop's home turned into an opulent palace of greed instead of a simple home for a man of God."

"What happened?" Morlanna asked.

"One day the men did not bring their gold. Instead, they called him into the graveyard to condemn him. Condemn him on holy ground."

"How dare you deny the church all you have promised," the bishop told them.

"It is you, Bishop, we deny. You have failed God, his people, and the dead," the first man said.

80

"If you wish for more gold ask the devil, as you'll not get another coin from us," the second man said.

"I would give my soul and the soul of any man knocking upon my door to the devil for the riches you possess," the bishop said.

Her hands began trembling. "Excuse me for a moment, I need another brandy."

Morlanna could see the woman was distressed. She stood. "I'll get it, you should warm yourself at the stove." She left the parlor, brought the bottle back, and filled Elsie's glass. "We can stop if you'd like."

Elsie took the brandy sipping it. "No. You need to know the whole story."

"Whenever you are ready."

Elsie sat down again, placing the brandy on the table for fear she might drop it. "When the bishop." Clearing her throat. "When the bishop offered his soul to Satan the ground beneath them shook, and his robes burst into flames. The men said he did not scream out in pain, instead began laughing as he walked away from them and into the palace. All of nature's life in the cemetery died before their eyes. The only birds you will find there now are crows."

"How did they have so much treasure to give?"

"It was pirate's treasure, Miss Miller," she answered, her voice trembling.

This story matched some of her research. The additional information about men with gold and a burning priest held her interest. "I'm sure they were mistaken about his robes bursting into flames."

She shook her head no.

"Things like that are not possible," Morlanna told her.

"This is not some yarn told to scare small children at night, Miss Miller. Every word I've spoken and secret divulged happened just as I said."

"Who were the men? Do you know their names?"

Elsie stood and moved near the stove. Then turned back, facing Morlanna. "I will not say their names in my home."

Morlanna rose, slowly approaching her. "Are you related to them?"

Elsie didn't realize she'd been holding the talisman the entire time. She took Morlanna's' hand, placing it in her palm. "The Bishop's Palace is corrupt.

I cannot tell you how many have entered, searching for the treasure said to remain inside. None have ever returned."

"You understand, I intend at some point to go there and see for myself what the Bishop's Palace truly is."

"Child, you must listen. The house reveals itself differently for those seeking its secrets. One person may see a grand home filled with lights and warmth, others a broken-down shamble inhabited by rats. The palace calls strongly for those wishing to enter. I beg you, reconsider, but if you go, take the talisman. Be strong in your faith, mark your way, or forever be lost." Elsie released her hands, walking away.

"Who are you, Ms. Elsie?"

"My given name is Boucet."

Morlanna tilted her head. "Boucet, Boucet." She took a breath. "You are related to Jean Laffite."

Nodding, she left Morlanna standing in the parlor.

She picked up the brandy, emptying the glass before moving quickly upstairs to make notes on everything said this evening. Her trip had turned into an adventure with a Voodoo Priestess casting spells and leaving a talisman. The possibility that Jean Laffite's gold built the Bishop's Palace would be a huge enticement for readers. Opening the window, she lit a cigarette and thought about what truly happened to Wilson. Did he make it to the Bishop's Palace or did the money of a rich woman pull him from the swamps? This would be another twist to add to her story unless he returned to San Francisco.

It was time to debunk all the stories by going to the palace. She would interview Mama Delphine afterward and return home with a story the entire world would pay to read. Morlanna smiled at the thought of finding a coin or two of pirate's gold to take home as a trophy.

Chapter 17

Saturday, October 4th

Morlanna could hear Ms. Elsie moving around the house, extinguishing the lamps room by room. She stood at the railing, thinking of their conversation three days ago, still confused about the statement to mark the way once inside the palace. The necessity to authenticate the story of the Bishop's Palace became imperative to avert question or speculation on the newspaper or herself. She felt Ms. Elsie could've provided more information, but the physical reactions were enough. She didn't feel it necessary to place the woman under further stress. Sadly, except for the name Boucet, Morlanna had nothing to prove the story was true.

She had received a notice from the livery stable advising there would not be a horse available until Saturday. This complicated a few things as she must time this trip precisely to be back and join Ms. Elsie for church services in the morning. Once the door down the hall closed, she took a cloak and lantern, moving quickly out the back door. Her habit of entering and exiting the house to smoke at all hours became routine and overlooked. The moon showed a quarter light, making her light the lantern.

She held it up so the individual waiting could see her face. "Hello there. I'm Miss Miller have you been waiting long?"

"No ma'am."

She walked up, handing him two coins. "You can pick the horse up at the boarding house around noon."

The young man nodded and waited until she mounted before hurrying away. She blew out the light and turned the horse in the direction indicated on Leotis' map. The animal sounds in the night began to disappear the longer she rode. When the horse refused to move forward, she dismounted, lighting the lantern again. Morlanna made a mental note to include the response of the horse and the lack of wildlife in the area. She followed the map through the trees, discovering the back gate of the cemetery. It was difficult to see if the stories of dead vegetation were true, but she would know more once the skies lightened come morning.

She wrapped the cloak around her shoulders and patted the derringer in her front pocket before proceeding through the gates. She stopped to look at the stone angels standing over the graves. They should have given a sense of peace and protection, but in the black of the night were unwelcoming. The outstretched arms offered a warning to hurry through and leave the dead unmolested. The decreased moonlight gave each headstone and crypt a ghastly presence. A sudden tug at the bottom of the cloak stopped her journey for a moment. The upraised hands covered in black mold and green moss immortalized the frail short life of a young girl. She removed the cloak edge from the hand, thinking a weaker individual might have taken it as an omen from those slumbering beneath her feet.

"Stone, nothing more Morlanna, just stone," she whispered.

The sound of a crow calling moved her forward toward the front gate. It moaned as she pushed against it to get free of the dead. The sight of two rusted cans almost destroyed by time caught her attention. If Wilson made it here, which she doubted, the containers could not have been brought here by him.

She raised her head and stood in awe of the magnificence of the palace, including the two-winged lions guarding the property. Its regal appearance made the dark stories she'd heard ridiculous. Any evil inside the palace came from the actions of men and proved the devil was human, not spiritual. Angels and demons held little sway in Morlanna's life as her father insisted there were answers to every question, including religion.

She stepped out into an open field and took a complete view of the entire area. There must have been a road here, at one time, as the bishop would have visitors on occasion. Her heart raced as she walked toward the building, surprised at the condition. The passage of time and weather hadn't affected its glory. The doors were magnificent and open, inviting her to cross over the threshold. The sight of a single candle burning on a side table answered all the questions.

"Lies and parlor tricks," she said, disappointed. At least now, all the nonsense would be put to rest. The sound of wood popping and a growing glow drew her forward. She wondered who would be waiting in the room, Ms. Elsie, maybe Leotis, and Cecile. Their trickery saddened and infuriated her.

"In here, Miss Miller," a voice instructed.

"Hello, who's there?" she asked, marching into the next room where a fire burned in a large ornate fireplace.

The wood on the wall was so dark it appeared black, bordered along the top with wallpaper of dark flowers and vines circling the room. She expected a familiar face but a single foot in a decorative slipper showed from the edge of a high back chair. The sight of a wrinkled and withered hand came to view on the armrest as she moved closer.

"Come in," the voice whispered.

"I demand you identify yourself and explain the disgraceful sham you have perpetrated on the town." No answer, only silence which angered Morlanna even more as it reminded her of Ludsworth. "Answer me!"

The deep raspy voice of a man answered. "Demand? Explain? You were allowed to enter my home and should be more gracious."

She laughed, crossing her arms. "Your home? I seriously doubt this house belongs to you, sir."

"Are you always so impertinent Miss Morlanna Miller?"

She reached in her pocket, placing a hand on the derringer. The individual rose from the chair in a bent manner and walked in front of the fire. He wore a long-tattered maroon dressing robe, a wisp of white hair on his head, and deep severe wrinkles gave him the appearance of a ninety-year-old man.

"I'm not sure how you know my name..." she said.

"I know many things about you," he told her.

"I do not know how it would be possible for a vagrant to know anything about me. You are pathetic taking residence here and using the legend of a demon bishop to scare men and boys away. I'm not sure how you have maintained this building, keeping it a secret from so many people. Do you have others helping you? I must admit it will make quite a story for people to read once it's written. I suggest you find another place to inhabit before I expose this charade."

He walked past her to a table where crystal glasses and decorative bottles stood. The man filled a glass with a dark liquid holding it toward her. When she refused, he smiled and moved back to the light of the fire.

"Do you not recognize me?"

"I see a miserable individual benefiting off a century of ghost stories. If you weren't so old, I would contact the authorities calling for your arrest," she answered.

"Such disrespect," he said, emptying the glass.

"How dare you speak of disrespect. You, sir, have no honor. I insist you identify yourself."

He smiled and raised a hand above his head. The bent stature became straight and tall. His white hair thickened, turning dark brown, while the deep wrinkles disappeared on his face and hands. The maroon dressing robe transformed, into the black and magenta cassock of a Catholic bishop, with an inverted cross of gold inlaid with jewels hanging around his neck.

"I am the Bishop, dear Morlanna. Welcome, to my home."

The transition shocked Morlanna, forcing her to step back into the wall. She turned to discover there was no longer an exit to the room. She began feeling along the wall desperately searching for a way out. When the intensity of his laughter increased, the derringer was pulled from her pocket firing both rounds into the bishop.

He looked down, puzzled at the two small holes in his cassock. "Did you truly believe a weapon would be effective?"

She dropped the gun, staring in disbelief. "No. This is not possible," she said and remembered Ms. Elsie's words. *"Mark your way."*

He walked over and took her hand, moving her into the light.

She looked up at him. "Are you going to kill me?"

He sighed. "Sadly, I am not allowed, but I can keep you."

"How long?" she asked, fearing his answer.

He moved into the high back chair and motioned for her to come close to him. "Since you have lost your way and your faith no longer has meaning in your life, forever."

Chapter 18

Mama Delphine

Estelle walked through her home upset with Anne-Marie for requesting they meet at such a late hour. This inconvenience added to her frustration over the inability to locate Mama Delphine since their last gathering. The priestess may have left the area or is hiding with one of her believers, and she refused to search the swamp for the woman's home. Mama Delphine seemed to know Estelle was looking for her and this made the promise to Elsie harder to honor.

She gathered two lanterns and a knife for protection against unwanted spirits of the bayou and left. The only things she wanted at this moment were a warm brandy and her bed, but the message said urgent. The familiar dirt road and night seemed unwelcoming, not even the frogs made any noise. She hadn't walked far when the figure of a woman ran toward her making Estelle reach for the knife.

"Stop! Are you a demon or friend?" She raised one of the lanterns, "Is that you, Anne-Marie?"

"Yes."

"You shouldn't run up on folks like that, scared me to death. Why didn't you wait for me at your house?"

"I know where Mama Delphine is," Anne-Marie told her.

"Where is she?"

"The Guidrys'. Cecile sent word to meet Leotis at the store. If he isn't there, we're to wait for him."

88

"Why in the world would Mama Delphine go out there? Cecile isn't a believer."

"I can't answer you. She said it was serious," Anne-Maire said.

"Then we should go."

They could see Leotis waiting in front of his store.

Ms. Estelle, Anne-Marie," he said and stepped down.

Estelle handed him her lantern. "Leotis, why is Mama Delphine at your house?"

He helped both women up into the wagon, joining them. "She showed up at dusk demanding Cecile send for you both. The woman has been burning sandalwood and hanging bells in the trees for two hours. She won't come inside the house, not that Cecile would invite her. Delphine said the small woman from the big city is in trouble and asked for you, Estelle."

Anne-Marie reached over, squeezing Estelle's hand. "We should stop and check on Morlanna?"

Leotis shook his head no. "Mama Delphine said to come straight back. We're not to stop or speak with anyone on our way."

"We should go then," Estelle said.

When they arrived at the farm, a fire blazed in the back of the house. They could see Mama Delphine walking around it. She wore white clothing with multiple pieces of beaded jewelry around her neck and arms.

"What is she doing?" Anne-Marie asked.

"I think it might be a blessing, can't be sure," Estelle said.

Leotis stopped the wagon helping both ladies down. "I'll go check on Cecile, then come out."

Mama Delphine stopped moving when she saw them arrive. "Leotis Guidry, bring your wife and strong coffee for all of us."

He nodded, moving quickly inside the house.

"Estelle, come here and bring the girl."

They moved toward the fire waiting for Leotis and Cecile. Mama Delphine placed a protective spell over everyone.

"Sit down and drink your coffee, there are things we must speak of," she told them.

"Why did you come here?" Cecile asked.

Mama Delphine drank her coffee, then spit in the fire. "All the trouble rising began here, at your home."

"I knew it. I told Leotis the moment Mr. Derby arrived, trouble followed him," Cecile said.

"Nothing you could do about it, Cecile. I saw the signs, hoped they would pass."

"Wilson Derby is in the palace, isn't he?" Leotis asked her.

"Yes. The weak-minded have no defense against it," she said.

"But Morlanna is not weak. She is strong, willful," Anne-Marie blurted out.

"It will not matter if she enters the palace," Mama Delphine told her.

"Why were you at Elsie's casting spells?" Estelle asked.

"Protecting my family, but there is nothing I can do for the small woman."

"I didn't know you had family," Anne-Marie said.

"Jean-Philippe is my brother. They are all I have left in the world, and I would die to keep them safe," she answered.

"You should have explained all of this sooner. Ms. Elsie is upset," Anne-Marie told her.

"I will child. There wasn't enough time for visits with all the work I needed to finish."

"Why did you bring us out here?" Estelle asked.

Mama Delphine threw sandalwood on the fire. "The small woman."

"Morlanna," Anne-Maire said.

Nodding. "She is in grave danger."

Leotis stood up. "The palace. She's going inside even after I warned her."

"We must stop her," Anne-Marie screamed.

Mama Delphine stood up and bent her head back, looking straight into the sky.

"What's happening Mama Delphine?" Estelle asked, reaching out.

Cecile moved into Leotis' arms silently praying.

"Estelle, is she okay. Why won't she speak?" Anne-Marie asked.

Mama Delphine raised her hands. "We are too late. The bishop has her."

"We must do something," Anne-Marie said.

"She is beyond our help," Mama Delphine explained.

"I won't accept that," Anne-Marie told her.

"Leotis, can you take us to Ms. Elsie's? Mama Delphine, you should come with us." Estelle walked over, comforting Anne-Marie.

Cecile looked up at her husband. "Go. I'll be fine."

"Cecile, go inside and stay until your husband returns. Don't be wondering outside no matter what you hear after we leave, understood?" Mama Delphine instructed.

She nodded, leaving them outside standing around the fire.

"Leotis Guidry, when you return home, the fire must burn all night, don't let the flames die." She handed him a small bag from her pocket. "Sprinkle a pinch of powder from the bag on each new log you place on it."

"How long should I keep it burning?" he asked.

"Until the sun shines on the flames, understand? Do it for your wife, good and evil are at war in our parish. We're all in danger," she told him.

"I will do as you say," he said, walking away.

The three moved away from the fire, then turned back, checking for Mama Delphine. "Go on, I have something left to do here before I can leave."

When she joined them in the wagon, Leotis turned back, looking at her. "My Cecile?"

"Safe inside the house. Do what I say, understood?" Mama Delphine asked.

Leotis nodded and drove the women back into town, stopping at the boarding house. "Ms. Estelle, will you be okay?"

She placed an arm around Anne-Marie as he helped them from the wagon. "We'll be fine. Thank you, Leotis. Get home to Cecile, we'll stay here tonight and figure things out tomorrow."

Estelle knocked on the door. It took a few minutes before they could see a light moving in the front rooms. Elsie opened the door in a dressing robe.

"What's happened?"

"Morlanna," Anne-Marie said.

"The bishop has her," Estelle said.

"Who else is with you?"

Mama Delphine stepped out.

"Priestess." She opened the door, stepping outside. "Come in, all of you."

Chapter 19

Saturday, November 1st
New Orleans

Ren wandered around the house, stopping to answer questions from the servants on the final preparations for the evening festivities. He usually was happy celebrating Dia de Los Muertos with friends from the city, but his thoughts were elsewhere. The feeling that something dreadful happened after their departure filled his soul. This dread had been noticed by more than the servants.

"Ren, why are you so gloomy? Your mood is affecting everyone in the house."

"You know the reason, Father. The problems associated with the Bishop's Palace would stop if we—"

Jena-Philippe held up a hand. "Not today! You will not disrupt tonight's celebration. If you were a child, I would lock you in your room. You will be cordial and courteous to our guests. I have invited several affluent men with daughters eligible for marriage."

"No, father."

"Yes. It is time for you to find a suitable woman and marry. These women are of proper breeding and will come with a high dowry."

"They are not cattle!" He turned to see the servants watching them. He lowered his voice, moving closer. "I will not marry for money."

"It is the only reason. A young man must plan for the future. Now, go prepare yourself, our guests will be arriving within the hour."

Ren walked away and upstairs to his room. His costume for the night lay across the bed.

"Sir," a male voice called from the door.

Ren smiled. "Bernard, come in."

"I have come to help you dress for the celebration."

He shook his head no. "I am forgoing the face decorations tonight, and can dress myself, thank you."

"If I may speak."

"Of course, speak your mind, Bernard."

"You have not been yourself since returning. Is it a woman? Are you in trouble?"

He grinned at Bernard, who had been his servant since childhood. "It's complicated, and there is a woman involved." He walked over, placing a hand on the older man's shoulder. "The trouble I am facing is an arranged marriage to a woman I do not love."

Bernard smiled. "I'll go help the others. It will be a long night for all of us."

Ren watched as Bernard shut the door behind him, and walked over to the window as the sunlight faded away. If Morlanna returned home, why had she not replied to his letter? He pushed away the feeling of concern and prepared for a night celebrating the dead.

It wasn't unusual for hosts to be late at parties, and he purposely took longer to join his father in the main room. The undecorated face would be a point of conflict between them the rest of the night.

The sound of music and laughter filled the house. His father appeared to have invited more than just a few men with daughters eligible for marriage. He slipped outside on the back veranda after several hours of boring conversation on the dance floor.

"Monsieur Ren," Bernard said.

"Yes. Is my father searching for me?"

"No. There are women at the front door asking for you."

"Women? Do they have an invitation?"

He shook his head, pausing, then looked down at the ground.

"Bernard, is there a problem?"

"Sir, Madame Delphine is with them."

Ren pushed past Bernard hurrying across the main room. His Aunt Delphine, Anne-Marie, Elsie, and Estelle, stood in the entry, dressed in travel clothing.

Elsie stepped forward, greeting Ren. "We apologize for the unexpected visit. It appears we have arrived at an inopportune time."

Ren moved to his aunt, kissing both sides of her face. "Nonsense, you are welcome in our home anytime."

Jean-Philippe walked toward the group followed by Bernard. "Ladies, welcome, come in and join the party. Ms. Elsie, lovely as ever."

"Father, Aunt Delphine is here," Ren said.

She walked around the ladies. "Jean-Philippe."

He bowed. "Delphine."

Estelle stepped forward. "Is there somewhere we can speak privately?"

"Yes, yes, my study is this way. Bernard, please see that their belongings are moved upstairs and have rooms prepared," Jean-Philippe said.

"We'll need some warm brandy," Ren told him.

"At once," he said, motioning for two women and two men to assist him.

They moved away from the entry into a room where a fire burned in the corner fireplace. Ren smiled as the ladies seemed impressed with his father's library.

"Ladies, please make yourself comfortable. I wish you'd informed me of your intentions. I believed we would be celebrating at Christmas."

"Jean-Philippe, hush. We are not here for a social visit," Delphine told him.

"Something has happened?" Ren asked.

Anne-Marie bit her lip and walked over, handing Ren the talisman. "She's gone."

"The bishop has her," Estelle told them.

Bernard entered the room carrying a tray of glasses and a bottle of brandy. "The rooms have been prepared for the ladies. Will there be anything else?"

"Ladies, can I get you some food?" Jean-Philippe asked.

"Possibly later, and thank you for allowing us to stay here," Elsie said.

"I would not have you stay anywhere else, nothing at the moment, thank you, Bernard," Jean-Philippe said. He poured brandy for them, then sat down in a leather chair by the fire. "Now, who has taken Miss Miller?"

"The bishop," Anne-Marie said.

"Nonsense," Jean-Philippe said.

Delphine stepped forward. "You celebrate the dead, or is it another excuse to drink. The woman is gone, my visions are true, and our family is to blame."

"And mine," Elsie added.

"How so?" Ren asked.

"The riches given to the bishop was pirate gold, stolen, and covered in blood," Elsie told them.

"Who gave him this gold?" Jean-Philippe asked.

"Lafitte," she answered, lowering her face.

"You are related to Jean Lafitte?" Ren asked.

"Yes, and I am ashamed to have his blood in my veins," Elsie told him.

"We must help her. Morlanna has been in the palace for a month," Anne-Marie said,

"Then she is dead," Jean-Philippe said.

"No," Delphine told him. "Imprisoned."

"What about the stories of those entering and never returned?" Ren asked.

"All men," Estelle told him.

"I don't understand," Ren said.

Elsie moved to the fireplace, her hands shaking. "It's part of the bishop's curse." She stopped, unable to continue.

Delphine walked over, placing both hands on her shoulders. "I give you the strength and safety in this house, to speak your truth."

Elsie nodded, composing herself. "The curse invoked by the bishop was on holy ground, and it involves taking the souls of only men."

"Not women?" Ren asked.

"No. Men refused to give him wealth," Elsie answered.

"Then there is a chance she's alive," Ren said.

"Yes," Delphine said.

"We have not located any entrance into the palace," Anne-Marie said.

"You have tried entering?" Ren asked.

"Day, night, it has made no difference. It does not change for us. No outside door will open." Estelle said.

"How did she get inside?" Jean-Philippe asked.

"Morlanna sought the truth, though never a believer in the story. Her faith was weak, and we believe he allowed her to enter," Elsie told them.

"Trapping her inside with no way to escape," Ren said.

"Yes," Anne-Marie said.

"If you cannot get inside, why did you come?" Jean-Philippe asked.

"We have a plan, but," Anne-Marie said.

"You need a man for it to work," Ren interrupted.

The four women all nodded.

"No, no, no. I do not believe any of this. I will contact the church, make a large donation, ask for a priest or bishop," Jean-Philippe said.

Ren stood up. "Father, money cannot fix every problem or correct our family's mistake."

"It could take months or years for something to be done, even if they believed you," Delphine told him.

"Why haven't you and your followers done something, sister?" he asked.

Delphine raised her eyes and walked over to Jean-Philippe, pointing a finger in his face. "You will not speak in such a disrespectful manner to me while you sleep, eat, and drink in my house. It is through my grace you are allowed to live in luxury, or have you forgotten who is first born and remains unmarried?"

Everyone in the room held their breath as the scene unfolded.

Jean-Philippe rose and bowed to her, not rising until he spoke. "Forgive me."

"It is my believers that feel there is still hope for Miss Miller. We can bring her back into the light but not without help," Delphine told him.

"What can we do?" Jean-Philippe asked

"Are there any official papers on the gift of land given to the priest?" Delphine asked.

Ren shook his head. "I have searched and can find nothing."

Estelle walked over, placing a hand around Anne-Marie's waist as her shoulders dropped. "We won't give up."

"Where did you search?" Jean-Philippe asked.

Ren pointed across the room. "In the large Amberg cabinet."

His father shook his head no. "Any gift of land or property to the church would be recorded in the family land ledgers."

Bernard entered the study. "Sir, your guests are asking for you."

Jean-Philippe nodded. "Ladies, come meet our friends, have some food and wine. The information we need will take time to find."

Anne-Marie walked over and hugged Jean-Philippe. "Thank you."

"Come, my friends, the food will be hot with the rich flavors of the city," Delphine told them.

"We'd appreciate the opportunity to freshen up after our journey," Elsie said.

"Of course, Bernard, please show them upstairs. Join us at your leisure, the celebration will last until morning," Jean-Philippe informed them.

As they left, he faced Ren. "I do not believe their story of ghosts, but I must honor Delphine's request."

"How many people must suffer because you fail to help them? Mother will never be at rest if we cannot end all of this. Where are these ledgers and how many are there?"

"They are in a storage room upstairs, the last time I saw them there were twenty, maybe thirty. Renaud, we must return to our guests, and later I want to know what makes you believe your mother is not at rest."

"I'll tell you now, she told me."

"You will not repeat that to anyone, especially the servants. You will never find a wife talking like a mad man. Now, come."

As his father left the room, Ren thought it strange he suddenly remembered there were ledgers in the house. He knew there would be a detailed notation of the gift to the church, and this might be the answer they needed. The Thibodeauxs' were a giving people but could be ruthless barons. After the arrival of the women and his aunt, Ren understood his uneasy feeling over not hearing from Morlanna. The images of what could be happening inside the palace were frightening. Was it possible for her to still be alive?

Chapter 20

Wednesday, November 19th

Ren walked down the stairs and into the parlor of the boarding house, still upset at his father for delaying their return. Jean-Philippe insisted the ladies remain to celebrate, and then the search through the ledgers took longer than expected. If it had not been for the assistance of Anne-Marie and Ms. Estelle, they would still be in New Orleans looking through eighty books in random order. They located information about the land he believed would help them but worried it would not be enough to free Morlanna.

The last action his father attempted before returning was a trip to the church to plead for assistance. The priest vehemently denied his request, calling him a blasphemer for even suggesting the church could be involved in such a scandal.

He walked into the dining room. "Good morning, Ms. Elsie."

She turned and smiled. "Is your father awake?"

"Awake and famished," Jean-Philippe said.

"Will any of the other ladies be joining us?" Ren asked.

"They'll be here shortly. I have breakfast waiting on the buffet and will join you momentarily."

The two men removed their plates from the table, filling them. She returned with tea and juice.

"I know of no place better in all of New Orleans which serves such a meal as this," Jean-Philippe told her.

She dabbed her mouth, blushing. "Thank you."

Ren glanced toward his father. "Ms. Elsie, would it be permissible to enter Morlanna's room?"

"I think you both should see it," she told them.

The front door opened. "Hello, good morning," Anne-Maire called out.

"We're in the dining room," Elsie said.

Ren rose from the table. "May I take your cloak.

"Thank you," Anne-Marie said.

"Would you take Jean-Philippe and Ren upstairs to Miss Miller's room? Please show them the items belonging to Wilson Derby."

"Who?" Ren asked.

"Wilson Derby is a work associate of Morlanna's who came here to prevent her from writing the story on the palace," Anne-Marie explained.

"Where is he now?" Jean-Philippe asked.

"Disappeared, leaving his clothes, the notebook, and a large amount of cash at the Guidrys," Elsie told them.

"Who sent Derby here?"

"Morlanna's boss, a man named Ludsworth," Anne-Marie answered.

"Leotis believes the bishop took Wilson," Elsie said.

"The bishop appears to be a busy man," Jean-Philippe said.

"Father!"

"It's fine Ren. We have no proof, but Wilson intended to burn down the palace. He arrived several weeks ahead of Morlanna asking questions around the parish," Anne-Marie said.

"The rest of the ladies will arrive at noon. You will have time to read over some of Miss Miller's research," Elsie said, handing Anne-Marie the key.

"Did Ms. Estelle obtain transportation for us?" Ren asked.

"Transportation? Are we going somewhere?" Jean-Philippe asked.

"We're going to the palace. I want to know a little more about the lure of a stone building, after you, Anne-Marie."

She led the two men upstairs, unlocking the door. Ren allowed his father to enter first watching his reaction to the displays on the wall.

"I don't think she will mind if you go through her papers," Anne-Marie told them.

100

"I have been wrong in my assumptions of Miss Miller, all of this is interesting," Jean-Philippe said.

"Morlanna is a wonderful person, smart, willful, and determined. We miss her terribly," she told them.

Ren picked up Wilson Derby's notebook allowing the money to fall out on the bed and looked at his father. "I doubt you would leave this amount of money for someone else to spend."

Anne-Marie nodded. "I'm going downstairs, please lock the room when you leave," she said, giving Ren the key.

Ren began scanning through a few pages of the notebook. His father continued to walk around the room.

"A mystery, wouldn't you say, Ren? Miss Miller and Wilson Derby may have run off together," Jean-Philippe suggested.

Ren raised his eyes from the notebook. "I don't believe she would be involved with someone like him."

"How can you be so sure?"

Ren handed the notebook to his father. "He has no honor, living off the money of others and pleased Morlanna might lose her job."

"This is a game. I cannot believe she is imprisoned in a crumbling building by a mythical bishop."

"You cannot deny the truth. The ledgers in your room prove the land was a gift for the priest to build a home."

"A small home, yes, not a grand palace. If any building still stands, it is on land not gifted or purchased by the church."

"Which means it belongs to our family, making him a trespasser and thief," Ren said.

The voices of women entering the house ceased their conversation. Ren locked the door behind them, joining everyone in the parlor.

"Is Mama Delphine here?" Clara asked.

"She and several ladies are meeting us at the palace," Elsie answered.

Ren looked at his father. "My aunt will be there? Why?"

"She believes you will not be able to withstand the pull of the palace unless we help," Elsie answered.

As Jean-Philippe began to speak, Ren stepped in front of him. "If Aunt Delphine feels we need her help, we'll be honored to have it."

Estelle arrived at noon, in time for a quick lunch. Ren and his father assisted the ladies up into the wagon. The women were eerily quiet as they traveled toward the palace. When the horses stopped, Estelle set the brake and then tied the reins to it while the women left the wagon.

"Why have we stopped?" Jean-Philippe asked.

"We walk, as the horses will go no further," Bernadette answered.

"The animals know a predator is near," Martine explained.

The group proceeded into a stand of trees, greeted by the sounds of crows. Ren looked at Anne-Marie when they arrived at the back gate of the cemetery.

"We aren't going inside, are we?" he asked.

"There is not another way," she told him.

"First, we leave a good road and are now forced through an old cemetery," Jean-Philippe complained.

Ignoring his comment, they entered the back entrance walking in single file. They could see Mama Delphine as they reached the front gate of the graveyard, standing next to six women dressed in white. As Ren stepped through the gate, he stepped in a pile of leaves and over several thick black vines. He looked down at his feet and noticed two rusted handles.

"Dear God," Jean-Philippe said at the sight of Delphine.

"Enough father, you must let this animosity of her beliefs go."

Ren watched as the women gathered around Delphine. He could hear her giving them instructions.

"Watch them closely. If they begin to act odd or not respond when addressed, we must intervene and remove both by force, if necessary," Delphine answered.

Ren turned to his father who seemed to be frozen, staring at the palace. He moved next to him and noticed the scent of sweet tobacco and observed the white smoke billowing from stone chimneys. He felt an increasing warmth and desire to move forward toward the palace. The two men began to walk away, ignoring the women screaming their names.

Jean-Philippe faced his son. "Renaud, we must greet the resident of this beautiful home."

"He must be a great man of standing and wealth."

"I expect there will be rich whiskeys and exquisite foods waiting for us inside," Jean-Philippe stated and straightened his jacket.

"I hope he has a daughter I might consider for marriage."

These were the last words spoken as they both slipped into deep darkness.

Chapter 21

Truths

Ren opened his eyes to the sound of women talking and the smell of lamp oil burning. He turned toward the voices and could make out Anne-Marie and Clara drinking tea. There was no daylight, and his body felt like something heavy lay on top of him. Ren found it difficult to focus clearly but knew he must be at the boarding house.

"What time is it?" he asked and moved slowly up in the bed.

They jumped up and ran over to him. "Clara, go tell Mama Delphine that Ren is finally awake."

He rubbed his head and looked at Anne-Marie. "What happened?"

A moment later, Jean-Philippe and the other women were at his bedside.

Mama Delphine handed him a glass filled with a terrible-smelling liquid. "No need refusing me, drink it, or I'll force it down you."

"Do it, son, it will make you feel better."

Ren held his nose like a child and swallowed the concoction. "I feel like I've drunk too much wine."

"Can you stand?" Anne-Marie asked.

He nodded, moving to the side of the bed, and continued to rub his forehead. "Did we enter the Bishop's Palace?"

Jean-Philippe looked into the eyes of the women. "We became bewitched."

"The palace cast a spell on both of you. It took all of us to keep you from going inside. We covered your heads and placed wax in your ears," Delphine told him.

Ren touched his ear, finding residue on it. "How long have you been awake?"

Jean-Philippe looked at everyone. "I awakened an hour ago. I have never felt the need or desire for anything as I did to enter the palace. It called to me, beckoning my very soul."

Ren took a moment to look at the faces surrounding him. "How can we fight something this powerful if it can control our minds and bodies to its will?"

"My son, I am afraid we cannot."

Ren dropped his head into both hands. "I will not leave Morlanna to this atrocious fate."

"We hoped together you might be strong enough to fight the enchantment of the palace in the daylight," Elsie said.

"We failed terribly," Ren said.

"I may have the answers you need."

Everyone turned to see Leotis and Cecile standing in the doorway.

"Word spread through the town of what you were attempting at the palace. I prayed you would be successful. We're here because you weren't," Cecile said, squeezing Leotis' hand.

"You've come to help us? Leotis Guidry explain your reasons," Delphine asked.

He looked at Cecile, then reached in his shirt pocket, pulling out a gold coin. "I have something which belongs to him and thought he might make a trade."

"How is it possible you have gold?" Ren asked.

"I thought no man had ever made it out alive," Anne-Marie said.

"Only one, my brother, Jimmie," Leotis said.

"I think Leotis has a story we need to hear," Delphine said.

As they made their way downstairs, the men brought chairs from the dining room into the parlor. Elsie brewed coffee instead of tea and whiskey-filled glasses this evening instead of brandy. A polite silence fell over them, waiting for someone to speak.

"Leotis, can you tell us what you know about the palace. How is it possible your brother made it out alive?" Ren asked.

Jean-Philippe interrupted. "Will he speak with us?"

Leotis dropped his head for a moment. "He passed."

"My sympathy, forgive me, sir," Jean-Philippe said.

"Jimmie was never right after coming back from the palace. His mind withered away from the experience and loss of two friends. The time has come for us to stop the bishop, or others will follow in Wilson Derby's and Miss Miller's footsteps. I can no longer bear the weight of innocent people losing their lives in that place."

"Did your brother tell you what happened?" Estelle asked.

Nodding. "Best he could, it always caused a great deal of distress recalling that night. As his time drew close, he told me everything."

"The stories around town said your brother never spoke after returning," Anne-Marie said.

"He didn't speak for almost a year. Our family felt it would be easier if we continued saying he couldn't so folks wouldn't bother him or ask us questions," he explained.

"Take your time Leotis," Elsie told him.

"May I see the coin?" Ren asked.

Leotis gave it to him. "The Bishop's Palace has always been a rite of passage for young boys. Most times, they barely get through the cemetery before turning around and running back home. A few brave ones have come close, feel the pull, but I intervene."

"Folks in the parish know you watch over the youth, stopping them from entering that foul place. I have boys of my own, always worrying they will hear the call, of the bishop," Martine told him.

"You have been near the palace?" Ren asked.

"Yes, many times," Leotis answered.

"It does not affect you like the others?" Bernadette asked, surprised.

Leotis shook his head no.

"You have some idea why I see it in your eyes," Delphine told him.

"The coin. I always carry it with me," he answered.

"Does it make you feel closer to your brother?" Delphine asked.

"I can't say, Mama Delphine," he answered.

"Tell us about him," Ren said.

"My brother was seventeen when he and two of his friends went out looking for the treasure hidden inside the palace. They made it through the cemetery just after dark. His friends left him standing at the gate, running across the field and up to the front door. Jimmie said they acted strange like they were under a spell."

"What about your brother?" Jean-Philippe asked.

"It didn't affect Jimmie in the same way. I can't tell you why, maybe because he never believed all the stories," Leotis answered.

"Your brother had a strong belief in God almighty and told me many times how he loved the Lord," Estelle said.

"Could be Ms. Estelle. I know every time the priest opened the church doors he went. My mamma said she believed it's one of the reasons he made it out of that place alive."

"Tell them the rest," Cecile encouraged him.

Leotis smiled at his wife. "Jimmie said they slipped inside, stopping at the smell of food. An old man dressed in holy clothes found them at the door and offered food, drink, and a warm fire for their company. As the night continued, my brother told the others they needed to head home. They refused to leave without gold or silver, proving the stories of the Bishop's Palace were true. An argument began over how they should search this huge house. The old man suggested they split up and search different areas."

"Didn't your brother think it strange for the old man to suggest they steal from him?" Ren asked.

"I asked him the same question. Jimmie couldn't give me an answer, he said it just made sense at the time. They all agreed it would be faster, but this turned out to be a bad decision.

"What about the old man?" Ren asked.

Leotis shrugged his shoulders. "After the suggestion, they split up he didn't speak another word to them. Jimmie told me in the beginning that every room in the house looked the same until he moved upstairs away from the center of the palace. He discovered a room with a decaying door that had no handle or latch. When he pushed the door open, the air smelled dusty, like no one cleaned it for a long time. There was a window on the far side, the only one he'd seen in the rest of the house. He could see dawn coming and started moving forward but stopped when it felt like there were rocks or pebbles beneath his feet."

"They weren't rocks, were they?" Ren asked.

"No. Gold and silver coins covered the floor beneath his feet, proving all the stories about treasure were true. Jimmie picked up a gold coin and turned to leave when the sounds of screaming stopped him. He became frightened, and instead of opening the window to escape, he kicked it out. The whole frame fell away from the building, wood splintered, and glass shattered everywhere. I never could understand how he managed to climb down without getting hurt. He always considered himself a coward for running off and leaving his friends inside to die.

"I cannot say I would not have done the same," Jean-Philippe said.

Ren felt Leotis was holding back. "Is there anything else you can tell us?"

Leotis looked at Cecile. "Tell them, my love," she told him.

"Jimmie didn't realize he'd placed the coin in a pocket until reaching the cemetery. The old man called to him from the broken window but in his mind. You may have escaped, but your soul will be mine.

"Excuse me for a moment," Jean-Philippe said, leaving the parlor.

"Ms. Elsie, all the treasure in the palace belongs to you," Leotis told her.

Ren turned to Ms. Elsie and handed her the coin. "I agree with Leotis."

Jean-Philippe returned with the ledgers calling everyone into the dining room. "I made an important discovery in our records."

Over the next two hours of discussion, Mama Delphine listened closely to everyone before speaking. "I believe Leotis, Elsie, and Jean-Philippe have the answers we need to end our problems with the bishop. Tell me the date of the gift? It would have been on a holy day."

Jean-Philippe took a minute to check the entry. "The eighth of December, the day of the Immaculate Conception."

"Does anyone know the name of the bishop?" Delphine asked.

"Is it important?" Leotis asked.

"Yes, it is," Delphine answered.

Jean-Philippe scanned both the ledgers. "There is nothing except the name of the parish priest."

"You will need to address the bishop by his formal name," Delphine told them.

"What if we can't find it?" Ren asked.

"It will make your actions difficult." Delphine glanced toward Elsie, moving closer to her. "You must reach deep inside and find that inner strength I know you possess. The success of our plan falls heavily upon your shoulders."

She closed her hand around the coin, nodding. "I always knew the blood Lafitte shed would be laid at my door one day."

Chapter 22

Monday, December 8th

Day of the Immaculate Conception

Morlanna could not remember the last time she'd slept in a bed or eaten a meal, though positive it was recent. The heavy gold-colored velvet dressing robe and matching slippers were comfortable though she could not remember changing clothes. She walked down the large ornate wooden staircase and looked back at the circular pulpit jutting out over the house. It represented the bishop's dominance over his flock and possessions. The foyer should have been at the end of the staircase, but today ended in the library. It seems nothing in the palace made sense.

There were rooms containing expensive furniture, plush rugs, and lavish draperies of gold and maroon. Curtains hung on walls where windows should be but were non-existent, including in her bedroom. Except for the library, the rooms on the main floor were all identical. The absence of windows made it impossible to know day from night or the number of days she'd been inside the palace.

She knew Wilson Derby had been imprisoned in the palace and couldn't understand why he remained secluded. Even the bishop didn't mention his name. The richness of this place would draw Wilson inside without question or hesitation disregarding any danger to himself. The missed opportunity to boast of good fortune and generosity bestowed by their host made his absence even more concerning.

"I thought you might like some tea," the bishop said, holding a silver tray.

She walked toward him, hesitating before picking up the cup. "It's not laced with poison, is it?"

He smiled, relaxing in a chair by the fireplace. "As I have told you many times since your arrival, I am not permitted to harm you."

"Yes, you keep reminding me, but why? Could you elaborate on this?"

"No." He motioned for her to sit down.

She took a seat across from him, not remembering a fire burning. "Why are there no servants?"

"Do you require a servant?" he asked.

She tilted her head. "No."

"You have food, drink, fresh clothing," he said, pointing at her robe and slippers.

"Again, would you like to elaborate on how this is possible?"

The bishop shook his head no.

"I understand Wilson Derby came for a visit. Is it possible for me to speak with him? It'd be nice to know he is well," she asked, sipping the tea.

The bishop leaned back in the chair, lacing his fingers together. "I'm afraid Wilson is no longer a guest of the palace. He was a very interesting individual, though inappropriately dressed the night he arrived to burn down my home."

"He told you of his intent?" she asked.

"My dear, men are happy to confess their transgressions once they've accepted my invitation of hospitality. Wilson Derby turned out to be no different and profusely apologized until his last breath. He laid all his actions at your feet."

"Ridiculous."

"Wilson described his suffering in the parish heat as your fault and said none of this would be happening if you had just stayed in your place. It appears your presence at work upset the boss."

"Milford Ludsworth is a disgusting excuse for a human." She took a moment before speaking again. "I assume since you said last breath Wilson is dead."

"Yes."

She cleared her throat. "Did he suffer?"

The bishop placed his chin on both hands. "Immensely, I do not take kindly to those who would take or destroy anything that belongs to me."

"I see."

He began laughing. "We will have many interesting conversations in the future."

She placed the teacup on a side table and leaned toward him. "I have no intention of having conversations of philosophy for eternity with you. There is a way out of the palace, and I will find it."

"I expected no less. Now, you must go upstairs and dress," he said, standing.

"Dress? For what reason?"

"We have guests coming. Your present attire is not appropriate to accept guests into my house."

"Why would anyone willingly come here knowing death lies within the palace walls?" she asked.

"I believe they are friends of yours. They think they will be able to free you from the palace."

Morlanna closed her eyes for a second, and he vanished. She walked to the fire, trying to understand why anyone would place themselves in danger, knowing there would be no escape? The people coming to the palace knew something she didn't.

"Think!"

Today must have a special meaning, possibly a holy day. The church granted special requests by parishioners and would receive gifts of influence during this time. The closest day of importance to the church was in December. She began to tremble and moved into the nearest chair to keep from falling.

"No, it can't be," she said.

"Morlanna."

She steadied herself on the arms of the chair before standing again. "I wanted to finish my tea. How long before our guests arrive?"

"You have two hours." He moved closer, taking her face in his hand. "You're concerned for these people? The only compassion you have ever exhibited is for yourself, why change now?"

She backed away from his touch. "You think I do not care for anyone? What proof do you have?"

"You used their friendship and hospitality to obtain information, ignored their warnings, and failed to recognize the pain they have endured. Your faith has failed if you ever had one. You belong here, with me, Morlanna Miller. The world is a better place without you in it. Go prepare yourself."

The weight of the robe seemed to increase in heaviness as she walked past him. The bishop's words lingered in her mind.

"I want you to greet our guests this evening."

She quickly turned around to face him. "I have no right to invite anyone inside the palace. Such action on my part would be inappropriate and distasteful under the circumstances," she said.

"It isn't a request. You will invite our visitors inside on my behalf."

"I require your full and proper title," she told him.

"You will acknowledge their presence and welcome them in the name of Bishop Maurice Solange Fabre as his honored guest. Morlanna, you will reconsider any thoughts of disrespecting my home or wishes, as I can be most disagreeable."

She acknowledged his threat. "May I ask a question?"

"Of course."

"What is the date?"

"Does it matter?"

She shook her head no. "I thought it might be a holy day."

Morlanna proceeded upstairs to her room, where the decision on her formal attire for the evening lay on the bed.

Chapter 23

Final Preparation

Over the past two weeks, the boarding house buzzed with people running in and out from sunrise to sunset. Mama Delphine took a room upstairs to stay close and available for everyone's questions. Elsie knew she remained to give her the assurance and support for the coming event.

She stepped back to take in a full view of herself. It had been years since she wore anything except black or dark colors. She ordered the emerald green sequined gown for the New Orleans holiday trip. The elbow-length gloves and feathers in her upswept hair matched perfectly. Elsie took a deep breath calming the nervous feeling inside, praying their plan would be successful. The hallway seemed long today, but the sight of two men in black front cut formal jackets, pants, white shirts, and vests, waiting on her in the parlor brought a smile.

Ren and his father bowed.

Jean-Philippe walked over, took her hand, and kissed it. "Magnifique."

"You look lovely Ms. Elsie," Ren told her.

She blushed. "If our plan is to work, I should look the part. Besides, if it doesn't, at least I will die appropriately dressed. Both of you look handsome and appear ready for the job ahead. Is Leotis here?"

"He hasn't arrived," Ren answered.

"I hope you gentlemen will not think badly of me, but I could use a brandy."

"Allow me," Jean-Philippe said and poured a sniffer for her.

"I think we could all use a drink," Ren said and filled two glasses with whiskey, giving one to his father.

Jean-Philippe raised his glass. "To our success."

She raised the glass, acknowledged the toast, and quickly drank the brandy. She heard the front door open and turned as Leotis joined them. He wore his Sunday suit, starched white shirt, and tie. She noticed his shoes were clean and polished though he seemed a little embarrassed by his appearance.

He looked down at his shoes and then faced them. "Cecile made me wear the suit. Is it proper?"

Ren walked over and shook his hand. "Yes, it's proper. Where is Cecile?"

"She left with Ms. Estelle at noon and said they will be waiting there for us," he answered.

"I obtained proper transportation for the evening. Delphine insisted we play the part even though we must walk part of the way," Jean-Philippe told them.

"I believe we should leave then," she told them and looked around the parlor as if it were for the last time.

"Do we have everything?" Jean-Philippe asked.

Leotis removed the coin from his coat pocket. "I am ready and do this for my brother and the parish."

Ren picked up the ledgers. "Yes."

Elsie opened her evening bag and removed a gold locket from it. "Mr. Thibodeaux, would you help me?" she asked and held the locket toward him.

Jean-Philippe took the necklace. "It would be my honor, Madame Boucet."

She placed a hand over it as he finished with the clasp. "I believe we are complete."

"Then we should go and meet our destiny," Jean-Philippe told them and picked up his top hat.

She looked at Leotis.

"Ms. Elsie be strong, Miss Miller needs you, the parish needs you."

She nodded. "I feel responsible for all of the things which have happened to this town."

Jean-Philippe stepped up to her. "Nonsense. The burden is not yours to bear. My family played a part in this issue, and we must do everything possible to end it."

As they left the house, she refused to look back, knowing their only choice would be to move forward. The ride to the palace was comfortable though silent. When the horses stopped, Jena-Philippe stepped out and assisted Elsie from the carriage. They were surprised at the number of wagons and horses standing in the field.

"What is all of this?" Ren asked.

"Cecile told me that Mama Delphine sent word to her female believers to come," Leotis told them.

"My sister must have contacted everyone in the parish and beyond," Jean-Philippe told them.

"I will welcome all the help they wish to offer," she told him.

Leotis stopped when they reached the gates of the cemetery. "Ms. Elsie, please allow me to help with your dress. My Cecile would be upset if it were to be damaged."

She nodded and thought of her unwarranted actions over the years to him, regretting them at this moment. If they lived, she would find a way to make amends to him and Cecile. "Thank you."

They made their way carefully through the cemetery exiting the front gate. Elsie turned to Jean-Philippe, who seemed shocked.

"What is all of this?" Jean-Philippe asked.

Ren moved next to his father. "Maybe we should go and ask."

They walked into a sea of women, young, old, Cajun, and creole, all seemed to be preparing for the conflict ahead.

"Some of these women are from the parish, but the others are unknown to me," Elsie told them.

"Cecile's sisters and their daughters are here," Leotis told Elsie.

The four joined Mama Delphine in the center of the group.

Ren approached his aunt. "How is this possible so many women have come?"

"Word spread of our plan to end the bishop's hold over the parish. One priestess from New Orleans arrived by train and brought thirty women. We will all work together to give you the strength to defeat this demon."

116

Leotis turned toward the setting sun. "It's time."

Jean-Philippe stepped forward, offering his arm to Elsie. She stood straight, accepting it. As they walked toward the palace, lights in all the windows began to glow. Flames exploded above the statues filling the area with light.

"I believe someone is expecting us," she told them.

"Father, how do you feel?"

"There is no effect, not like before, and you?"

"Nothing," Ren answered.

"Leotis, are you with us?" Elsie asked.

"I have God on my lips and gold in my hand. This evil does not affect me," he answered.

Elsie squeezed Jean-Philippe's arm. "This is the first time since we began this plan that I actually believe it may work."

As they walked toward the door, she could hear Leotis whispering the Lord's prayer behind her.

The Palace

The concept of time meant nothing inside the palace, she thought, looking up into the mirror of a dressing table. Her last thought was entering a tub of steaming water to bathe. Morlanna could not remember dressing or styling her hair with the heavy combs of gold and jewels. The dark colors of shadows, thick eyeliner, and maroon lipstick reflected the image of a stranger. The indecent neckline of the heavy beaded maroon gown would never have been a personal choice.

When the bishop called to her from the other side of her bedroom door, she shivered.

"It's time Morlanna, let me in," he said.

She opened the door, stepping slightly to the side allowing the bishop to enter. She felt unclean as he stood staring down at her.

"Appropriate, but not complete," he said and opened a velvet box containing a large gold ornate ruby necklace and earrings.

"I cannot accept this," she said.

"It is not a request, turn around," he demanded.

She trembled as he placed the necklace around her neck. "It's a little much for me."

"I don't believe it is, and you will need these," he said, handing the earrings to her. "Our guests are walking up the stairs. Please go and greet them, do not forget our earlier conversation."

She walked past him and placed the earrings on, turning back to discover he'd gone. The knock at the door forced her out of the room and down the staircase. For the sake of the people on the other side, Morlanna would do as the bishop instructed.

When she reached out for the handles, the sight of black full-length silk gloves made her frown. How can I do this? I can't let someone else die or become a prisoner."

"No, I won't do this. Do you hear me, bishop?"

His voice rang throughout the palace. "Morlanna, if you do not open the door, I will kill all of them where they stand."

"Your powers are contained inside the palace. I do not believe you," she said.

"Are they? Shall I kill the young man to prove how far-reaching my powers can be?"

"Stop, stop!"

"Open the door and invite them inside."

Chapter 24

The Invitation

The massive doors to the palace opened, Morlanna heard Elsie gasp as she greeted them and observed Jean-Philippe hold up a hand preventing Ren and Leotis from moving forward. It was hard to face the people who came to save her, unsure if they would be allowed to leave unharmed. The sound of the bishop clearing his throat encouraged her to move into the threshold, preventing them from entering without his invitation.

She felt like a marionette when both of her arms opened wide as if to embrace them. "On behalf of his grand and gracious holiness, the Bishop Maurice Solange Fabre, I bid you welcome. The bishop asks that you freely accept his offer of hospitality."

Jean-Philippe removed his top hat and bowed. "We accept Bishop Fabre's gracious invitation and generosity."

Morlanna stepped back and allowed them to enter the palace. As the doors closed, the sound of women chanting made her stop and listen. She believed it was her imagination, hearing nothing further. They walked into a large foyer where the bishop's booming voice drew everyone's attention upward toward the pulpit-shaped balcony.

He held his hands out toward them. "Welcome sinners to my home."

She watched as they stepped back, taking in the sight of the impossible. The bishop stood before them, in physical form, dressed in formal vestments, including a white and gold Quora. He held a gold staff topped with a large inverted jeweled cross, and rings of gold inlaid with jewels gleamed on his fingers.

"God save us," Jean-Philippe said.

She could see Ms. Elsie's hand tighten on Jean-Philippe's arm and Leotis stepped next to her crossing himself for protection.

The bishop laughed and descended the staircase. "God cannot help you inside the walls of my palace."

Jean-Philippe straightened his posture and looked toward Morlanna before he spoke. "We request an audience, your eminence, on this holy day of Immaculate Conception."

"There is important business that needs discussion," Elsie told him.

The bishop stopped next to Morlanna. "Business, not pleasure?" he asked, placing a hand on her shoulder.

She watched Ren control his actions and knew Jean-Philippe warned him to be respectful, regardless of the situation.

The bishop smiled. "Come inside, Morlanna will see to your needs."

She stepped forward taking Jean-Philippe's hat and lead them into a large room where a blazing fire gave an immense glow. A banquet table stood filled with food, a number of them steaming as if just removed from the oven. Elsie released Jean-Philippe's arm and walked to a small buffet where a large decanter of brandy stood, picking up a glass.

Morlanna moved quickly to Elsie's side, removing the glass from her hand. "Accept nothing from him, or be imprisoned with me forever."

"Morlanna!" The bishop said, entering the parlor minus the formal vestments. His simple maroon cassock matched her dress, with a long gold chain hung around his neck displaying the inverted cross.

When he turned away, she whispered. "Accept nothing."

"Do you know why we have come?" Jean-Philippe asked.

The bishop poured wine into a golden chalice and then walked past them to a high-backed gold velvet chair in front of the fireplace. He sat down and raised a hand signaling for Morlanna to move next to the chair.

"I assume you have taken the day of Immaculate Conception to request her release. Your research on the holy days is impressive as they alter certain aspects of my powers. My compliments, you are the first not to be influenced by the palace." He reached over, taking her hand.

She realized he lied, making her responsible for their entry into the palace. She leaned down so the others could not hear. "You lying bastard."

He smiled and kissed her hand. "I feel you have wasted this opportunity for grace. You see, I have grown extremely fond of Morlanna. She brightens the dark hallways of my home and is a worthy adversary and conversationalist. I am not permitted to take the life or soul of any woman however; I can imprison them forever. My generosity for this holy day will not include her freedom, but I will allow you to leave unharmed."

"You have mistaken our intentions, Bishop Fabre. We have come for another reason besides the release of Miss Miller," Jean-Philippe told him.

"Why would you enter my home if not for my mercy?" he asked.

Morlanna watched as Leotis stepped forward, removing a gold coin from his pocket, and held it up for the bishop to view.

"I have gold taken by a man whose soul you never claimed."

The bishop released her hand and leaned forward in the chair smirking at Leotis. "A foolish boy once escaped with my gold and his soul. Tell me, Leotis Guidry, did your brother die peacefully or in pain from the experience which haunted his days? You are naive to think one piece of gold would free anyone. I will take it back and decide whether you will leave my home untouched," the bishop said, reaching out.

At this moment, Elsie stepped forward, taking the coin Leotis held up to the bishop. He leaned back in the chair. "This gold has never belonged to you."

He drank from the challis. "Who are you, besides a showcase for these men? Shall I keep you, too? What right do you have to my gold?"

Morlanna watched Ms. Elsie turn to Jean-Philippe, who nodded, and Leotis moved back behind her. A breeze blew through the room as Ms. Elsie stepped forward closer to the bishop, removing the necklace. When the locket was opened, the curtains began to move making a sound similar to ship sails being raised. She turned the locket with a photograph toward him and held up the coin.

The bishop immediately recognized the photograph and threw the challis across the room spilling wine on the floor. "No!"

"I, Elsie Marguerite Boucet, am the descendant of Jean Lafitte and in his name, have come to reclaim his fortune given to you, Bishop Maurice Solange Fabre." The wind increased, fanning the flames of the fire and surrounding her. "No gold or silver will you keep all treasure you possess will be returned to my family. You dishonored him, the dead, and people of the parish, failing to keep your promise to God on holy ground."

The bishop was pulled out of the chair, as the heavy gold chain and cross broke free from his neck. He stretched out both hands to grab the chain, and the rings flew off his fingers, landing at Elsie's feet as if she were a magnet. Morlanna's neck, chest, and ears began to bleed as the jewelry tore away from her body. She quickly removed the heavy combs, throwing them to the ground to avoid having them painfully pulled out.

The bishop began to scream and point first to Ms. Elsie and then to the right of her. Morlanna blinked at the sight of a man standing next to Ms. Elsie dressed in clothing from a time past, including a plumed hat. She called to Jean Lafitte, and he had answered.

"No! Woman, you have no power or right to the treasure given to me. He and the others begged me to stay, promising this wealth. I remained as they asked!"

Morlanna realized they were there to both rescue her and save the parish. As the wind increased, the house shook, and the ceiling dropped gold and silver coins on the floor like rain. Jeweled chalices', platters, and swords, tumbled down the stairs carried by the wind all landing at Ms. Elsie's feet. She watched as the woman continued to stand defiant in front of the bishop with Jean Lafitte, remaining at her side.

Ren stepped forward, fighting against the wind, holding the ledger firmly. He forced it open where a red ribbon marked the day. "In the name, of my family, I, Renaud Pierre Thibodeaux, remind you, Bishop Maurice Solange Fabre, of my ancestor's gift. On this holy day, the parish priest received one acre of land to build a simple home. A true man of God, one who fulfilled his promises to the people of the parish and the dead. I admonish you for your failures to the church and these people."

The bishop pointed his finger at Ren. "I accepted what they offered, these are lies and I will not listen. If you do not stop, I will send all of you to hell!"

Morlanna moved away feeling along the walls and turned her head, trying to avoid the increasing wind. She could see Jean-Philippe slowly moving to Ms. Elsie's left holding a book. His words were difficult for her to hear but powerful.

Jean-Philippe opened the book where a gold ribbon lay, turning it toward the face of the bishop. "This abomination has been built with the hands of good and decent men on stolen land. You are a thief, Bishop Maurice Solange Fabre. In the name of my ancestor Fran-Pierre-Renaud-Philippe Thibodeaux, I, Jean-Philippe Thibodeaux, demand you leave the land to which you have no claim. You are banished to live on the one-acre given freely in the love of our Lord to the parish priest, whom you dishonored before God on holy ground. You will leave this land before the sun shines upon this place."

She reached the opposite side of the room next to Ren and Leotis. The locket and coin seemed to be shielding them from the worst of the bishop's wrath. The comb in Ms. Elsie's hair no longer held the style and the dress became damaged by flying debris. They darted away from moving furniture, blowing across the room, avoiding decanters of brandy and crystal glasses shattering on the floor. The dark wallpaper pulled away as the walls began to crumble around them.

Ren placed an arm around her as they watched the bishop tear at his vestments. She could see his body aging as the palace deteriorated.

Elsie turned her head toward them. "Go!"

Leotis took Morlanna's arm and yelled in her ear. "Where is the door?"

"If I knew, I would have left," she told him.

"We must find a way out, or the palace will kill all of us," Ren said.

They ran into the foyer, but the door no longer existed.

"Upstairs," Morlanna told them.

"Wait. What is that sound?" Ren asked.

The wall in front of them began to crack from ceiling to floor.

"Someone is pounding on the wall," Leotis told them.

"With what? A battering ram," Ren asked.

The stained-glass windows shattered as wood splintered forcing Morlanna to grab both men by their jackets. "Move back!"

The wall fell into a pile of rubble and left a large opening for them to escape. Delphine yelled from the outside. "Here, hurry, hurry, dawn is coming."

Morlanna could see Cecile standing behind Delphine. "Leotis go, your wife is waiting."

He looked at Ren, who nodded in agreement. "Hurry all of you." He jumped through the opening into Cecile's waiting arms, looking at the sky. "How is it possible?"

"Come, we must leave this place. I'll explain later," Cecile told him.

She turned back to see Ms. Elsie and Jean-Philippe facing the bishop. "We cannot leave them."

"They must finish this together," he said, taking her hand and pulling her out of the palace.

They ran down the stairs and into the field turning back, waiting for the others. She barely noticed Anne-Marie wrapping her in a quilt.

The Bishop's End

Elsie couldn't bear much more of the bishop's wrath and turned to see Jean-Philippe checking on the others. She prayed they were out of the palace.

He placed an arm around Elsie's waist and leaned close to her ear. "Madame Boucet, it is time to go. We have completed our task."

Elsie nodded and then felt as if a hand touched her right shoulder. She looked but did not see anyone. They moved quickly out of the room when a horrific scream made them look back. The bishop stood engulfed in flames, the skin peeling away from muscle and bone dropping to the floor. There would be no laughter this time, just eternal torment. The bishop moved toward them with outstretched arms.

Jean-Philippe grabbed Elsie, pulling her through the opening in the wall. The sound of windows breaking and iron bending filled the air as the palace began to fall into rubble. Both winged guardians dissolved into ash enveloping them in a cloud of dust and debris. In the midst of the uproar,

Elsie heard Morlanna screaming her name. When the air cleared, she stood trembling, wrapped in the arms of Jean-Philippe, battered but alive.

"Are you hurt?" Ren asked running up to them.

Jean-Philippe raised his hand. "We are good, son."

"How is Morlanna?" she asked.

"Alive, confused."

Elsie raised her head from Jean-Philippe's shoulder. "You need to go and help her understand."

"I'm not sure I can do that," Ren told her.

"You must try," Jean-Philippe told him.

Ren glanced back and could see Anne-Marie wrapping her arms around Morlanna. "I don't know if I am the right person to do this."

Elsie pushed the hair from her face and looked at him. "I believe you are."

Ren nodded.

Lost Time

Morlanna closed her eyes and tried to focus as everything seemed to be spinning. The ground felt unstable as if she'd awakened from a nightmare and stumbled out of bed. It took a few moments to see all the women standing in the field. The cold breeze blowing across her arms and chest brought a realization the seasons had changed. She could see Anne-Marie reaching out.

"We never thought we'd see you again."

She stepped back. "Anne-Marie, is it true?"

Ren walked up as Morlanna asked the question.

Anne-Marie looked up at Ren. "It, Ren, I can't tell her."

She faced Ren. "Is it true, the date?"

"Morlanna, maybe you should—"

She took his hand. "I have to know, please someone tell me. Is it the day of Immaculate Conception?"

He sighed. "Yes."

She stumbled back a few steps, pulling the quilt tighter around her body. "How is it possible so much time has passed?"

"What can we do to help you?" Anne-Marie asked, almost in tears.

She shook her head. "I'm going to need some time to pull all this together in my mind. It seems as if I had been in there only a few days. Ren, I didn't want to let you or anyone else inside, but he threatened to kill everyone if I didn't follow his orders."

Mama Delphine walked up, hearing Morlanna. "Child, none of this is your fault. We should have stopped the bishop long ago. It took you being imprisoned for the rest of us to come together."

"Who are all these women?"

She smiled and spread her arms out. "They came from many places, bound together with a strong will and belief their strength could bring you back. A well thought out plan executed by good people has ended the evil in our parish."

"How can I ever thank all of them, all of you?" she asked.

"No need. Let's get you back to the house and out of those rags. This land will need time to heal," Delphine told her.

Morlanna looked down at the dress disintegrating before her eyes.

Chapter 25

Friday, December 12th

Morlanna straightened the skirt and blouse, staring at the reflection. The past few days felt like a terrible nightmare with pieces of her memory missing. She remembered arriving back to the boarding house wrapped in a blanket and nothing more. Estelle, Anne-Marie, and Clara brought food upstairs, filled the tub with hot water, and seemed overprotective as the experience made her sleep fitful. Clara checked in around midnight to discover her sitting on the windowsill smoking in nothing but a sheer robe with a cold north wind blowing. She thought about their conversation just a few hours ago.

"Morlanna, are you okay?"

She took a long draw before throwing the cigarette out the window. "Do you know what he said?"

"Who are you talking about?"

She shut the window and faced Clara. "The bishop. He told me the world would be a better place without me in it."

"That isn't true. He said those terrible things in the hope you would question your self-worth. When a person's self-esteem becomes shattered, it can imprison them."

"Was he right about me not caring for anyone else's pain or misfortune?" Morlanna asked.

Clara took her hands. "I don't know what your life was like before you came here, but I never saw that in you. There are times in everyone's life when it becomes

127

necessary to take a hard look in the mirror. If you're not happy or see something you dislike, change it."

She nodded. "I hope it isn't too late."

"If you are still breathing in the morning, it's not too late. I'm going downstairs for a cup of tea. Can I bring you something?"

She smiled. "I would love a big piece of pie or cake, anything sweet.

"One piece of blueberry pie coming up."

Morlanna looked over at the empty plate and fork on the side table, hoping there would be more pie in the kitchen. As the door opened, she could hear Ren's voice talking to someone downstairs.

"Good morning," Elsie said, taking the plate and fork.

She looked at Ms. Elsie's noticing the severe hairstyle was gone, replaced with soft curls framing her face. The woman looked radiant in the bright colors of a green and yellow checked dress. Her eyes seemed brightened by the smidge of mascara, and did she see lipstick? Morlanna realized the past few days seemed to have changed more than just her life.

"I thought another piece of blueberry pie would be nice for breakfast."

Everyone began laughing. "I'm afraid the only pie left is apple. Ren finished the blueberry," Anne-Marie told her.

"It's good seeing you up, please, excuse me," Jean-Philippe said, following Elsie into the kitchen.

She looked around the table at everyone smiling as Jean-Philippe left. Morlanna felt like she'd missed a large part of the story but wasn't ready to ask for more information.

"It appears you have something on your mind," Anne-Marie told her.

She shook her head no. "I'm trying to understand and accept the time I lost, and the reality of the palace."

Ren stood up and pulled out a chair next to him. "It will take some time adjusting to the things you experienced, as it did father and myself. On an earlier attempt to enter the palace we became affected and would have become victims if not for these ladies saving us."

"With all the time that has passed, I should contact my family and landlord. They will all be worried. I don't know if I'll ever be able to tell them the reason," she said.

"Tell them you met a mysterious man from New Orleans," Anne-Marie told her.

Morlanna glanced at Ren.

"I am happy to be your excuse for being delayed," he said.

"We have some news. Jean-Philippe and Ren are staying for the holidays," Bernadette said.

"Say you'll stay, Morlanna," Anne-Marie begged.

"Yes, be here with your new friends on Christmas," Clara added.

"I understand the weather is dreadful in the direction you will be heading," Ren said.

"I'm not sure it's possible, with the story to write about my experience, and I need to tell someone what happened to Wilson." Morlanna stopped talking when Ren placed his hand on top of hers. She looked over at Clara shaking her head, no. What was she doing? These people put themselves in danger for her, and she intended to run away, again. The time had come for her to stop and look at the people who were truly important. "You know what, I think spending the holidays here is a grand idea. Yes, I will stay."

Ren picked her hand up and kissed it as a small cheer rose from the table.

Elsie and Jean-Philippe returned to the dining room.

"It's warm," Elsie said, handing her the pie.

"Morlanna has decided to stay through the holidays," Anne-Marie said.

"Wonderful. Café?" Jean-Philippe asked.

"Coffee, there's coffee?"

He nodded.

"Yes, please," she told him.

Mama Delphine opened the front door, entering, followed by Estelle, Martine, and a north wind.

"Good morning, ladies," Jean-Philippe said.

"A little too cold for me," Delphine told him.

"Then why go out, sister?" Jean-Philippe asked.

"We had things which needed checking," Delphine told them.

"And what was that?" Ren asked.

"The palace," Delphine said.

"I thought you said the land needed time to heal," Morlanna told her.

"True enough, and when the spring comes, we'll know for sure. A crow landed on my windowsill this morning, a bad omen," she told everyone.

The room fell silent. Estelle held up her hand. "No need fretting, everything is fine."

"I'm not sure fine is the correct word. Strange comes to my mind," Martine said.

"Ladies, please be a little clearer," Ren told them.

"We went out there, and the horses walked almost into the tree line. The black paint on the cemetery gates is falling away. It will need a new color come spring," Estelle said.

"Can't tell about the trees, hopefully, they'll bud out after winter. All those thick black vines running everywhere are shrinking. We walked out where the palace stood," Delphine said.

"I'm telling all of you what we found is strange," Martine said.

"Has something changed at the palace?" Anne-Marie asked.

"It's gone," Estelle said.

"Gone?" Morlanna asked.

"Yes, gone. There is nothing left, not a stone, piece of wood, glass, or metal railing," Delphine said.

"Impossible," Jean-Philippe said.

"Leotis and the men must have cleared it all away," Elsie said as an explanation.

"How'd he get wagons in there? I don't believe anyone can move those big stones through the gates. Something happened out there after we left, I can't explain it," Delphine told them.

Morlanna ate the apple pie and savored the coffee, pretending she wasn't interested in the story.

Ren turned and looked at her. "I know what you're thinking, and it's not a good idea, not now."

She made a face at him. "I do have a question for Mama Delphine."

"Go ahead."

"You said there was a plan. How did you know they were successful?"

"The outside wall began cracking and falling on the outside, and then we heard the wind blowing," she explained.

"What did you use to break down the wall?" Ren asked.

Mama Delphine looked puzzled. "Cecile and I just pushed it down with our hands. It wasn't much more than dried clay or mud."

"It sounded like you were ramming it with a big tree," Morlanna told her.

"Nope, just our hands."

Ren shook his head.

"It appears there is nothing to see or worth any more of my time. I do need to go into town and send some telegrams. Ren, would you accompany me?"

Ren smiled. "It will be my honor. I need to stop by the church and light a candle for mother."

"I just thought about something. Why didn't the parish priest come and help you get rid of the bishop?"

Delphine began to laugh. "Child, this parish hasn't had a full-time priest since the one died in 1815."

"A different priest comes for services, but no one will accept this parish," Martine added.

The church knew and did nothing to help these people. She frowned and started to speak when Jean-Philippe stepped up to the table.

"Then it is time for all of that to change. I will speak with the bishop in New Orleans and ask that the spiritual needs of this parish be met," Jean-Philippe said, handing Morlanna an envelope.

"What's this?"

"I have a good friend at the *Times-Picayune*. He is interested in your work and anxious to speak with you," Jean-Philippe said, smiling.

Chapter 26

Wednesday
    April 8th, 1891

Morlanna walked into the sitting area of the private train car. She and Ren were returning to see friends and make a final visit to the place where the Bishop's Palace stood. A new year, a new job, and a new life began after leaving her friends, thanks to Jean-Philippe. The introduction and meetings with the owner of the *Times-Picayune* in New Orleans had been delightful. Their lengthy conversation about employment was intense with her insistence, that the newspaper pay for relocation. She would write an exclusive four-part series on the Bishop's Palace, including its destruction. Her relationship with Ren blossomed along with everything else in her life.

"Café?" Ren asked.

"Yes, thank you," she told him and wrinkled her nose.

He filled a cup handing it to her. "What's wrong?"

"I never realized how strong the smell of cigars and cigarettes were until I stopped smoking."

Ren laughed. "I never understood why you felt the need for them."

"In the beginning, they proved I could be part of the club, then it became a crutch," she explained.

"A crutch you never needed in my opinion. How do you feel about returning to see everyone, nervous?"

She took a sip of the coffee. "I believe curious would be the word. It can't be any harder than walking into Ludsworth's office with Wilson's notebook."

"I think you were a little dramatic pouring the bottle of red ink on his desk and then blaming him for Wilson's death."

She smiled. "Wilson may have been many things, but I cannot imagine his horror realizing he was about to die. No, Ludsworth deserved my wrath and has blood on his hands. If it were not for the four of you so would mine."

"I thought he might attempt some legal action forcing you into completing the story for the paper. I contacted the family lawyer before we left and acquired his services should we need them. It appears you had a better plan."

"Ludsworth refused to give me any money except for salary. I financed the entire trip, and he never promised to print the story. With Wilson's notebook in my possession detailing their conspiracy, there wasn't much he could legally do."

"I'm sure he has regretted that decision. How many papers did the *Times-Picayune* sell with your exclusive?"

"I shouldn't brag, but the newspaper made several donations to local charities with the additional reprints of the story."

"My favorite part of our trip was meeting the Montgomery's."

"I hated to see her cry when we packed up my room."

"It was a nice gesture giving Wilson's five hundred dollars to them."

"I don't think he would mind. They are good people and can use the money."

"I certainly enjoyed the basket of food she gave us the day we left."

Morlanna shook her head. "I swear the woman cooks all the time and seems to give more away than keep. Did you enjoy meeting my family?"

"I must admit speaking with your father had me on edge, and I'm still nursing sore ribs from your brothers. It seems while you have been away, the family expanded. How many grandchildren are there?"

"Too many for me to count. How do you feel about being the best man for your father?"

Ren shook his head. "I always thought it would be one of the other ladies."

She laughed. "Anne-Marie or Clara, you mean? They are too young, Ms. Elsie is the right choice."

"Father informed me he is having a home built so they can spend time in both the town and New Orleans. I believe it is almost finished."

133

"I didn't think he would ever come back and stay after everything that happened."

"He believes it would be too hard on Ms. Elsie to suddenly uproot her from everyone."

"Your father didn't build their new house where the palace was, did he?" she asked.

"No, on the land he bought last year. Did I tell you father received a personal visit from the Bishop of New Orleans?"

She raised her eyebrows at him. "The one who married us last week?"

"Yes, that bishop."

"When? And why didn't you say something before now?"

"I was afraid you wouldn't let him do our ceremony. His visit took place while we were in San Francisco. The bishop announced the recent increase in correspondence from parishioners required his attention. His superiors instructed him to advise the church and the holy father in Rome denied such things were possible or took place. Privately, he could not be more thankful this nightmare had ended. The original acre of land has been returned to our family with Romes' blessing."

"What about a new priest?"

"Arrived a few weeks ago. The town built a home next to the church before his arrival."

"What about the boarding house?" she asked.

Ren smiled. "After the wedding, Anne-Marie will be the proprietor until she no longer wishes or moves away."

"I've missed everyone terribly. Ren, promise me we will come back often."

He pulled her into his lap. "If I can drag you away from your charity work, we'll come back anytime you wish."

The train pulled into the station, allowing them to step out into the sunshine and the smiling faces of the Guidrys'.

Ren shook Leotis's hand. "I thought my father would meet us."

"We're escorting you to see him and Ms. Elsie," Leotis said.

Morlanna walked over to them, arm in arm with Cecile. "Problem?"

"We're going on a ride," he told her.

134

"Any place special?" Morlanna asked.

"Jean-Philippe said there is something you both should see," Leotis told her.

"I love surprises, and it's a beautiful day for a ride," she told them.

As they drove down a familiar road, it split into different paths. Leotis pulled the wagon to the left.

"This is new," Ren told him.

"Much has changed since you left us. We have a new road for easier access to the cemetery."

Leotis stopped in the front of the cemetery that once faced the palace. Ren and Morlanna walked toward the iron gate gleaming white with the green leaves of trees swaying gently in the breeze. The vines were gone, replaced with multicolored flowers blooming everywhere in the cemetery making the air smell sweet. The black mold and green moss no longer clung to headstones or statues. The birdbaths throughout the area were filled with different species singing and chirping.

She wrapped an arm around Ren. "I believe your father has been busy with these improvements."

They turned, walking out into a field of tall grass where Jean-Philippe and Ms. Elsie sat on a blue patched quilt drinking wine. Morlanna smiled when he leaned over and poured wine into several glasses kissing the woman on her cheek. She thought Ms. Elsie had grown younger-looking and believed it could be from her happiness.

Ren looked at her and laughed at his father's actions. "He's always enjoyed the company of women in the past, but this seems different to me."

"He's genuinely happy, no pretense. Can't you see it?"

"Father."

"Ren, Petit welcome," he said, standing to greet them. "Is this place not amazing?"

She walked away mesmerized by the changes in the land. Death and darkness were replaced by life, with cattle grazing and flowers blooming. The birds singing made her relax, knowing the bishop was truly gone.

Ren joined her. "Leotis told me once winter ended, the land began changing, healing itself."

"Who owns all the cattle?"

"Leotis. The land is his to use, father's gift for the strength he showed in the palace."

She motioned for him to come closer. "I do have a question about Ms. Elsie demanding the bishop return his wealth to her family."

"Did she escape with any of the treasure from the palace?" Ren asked.

"There seemed to be a lot of it coming from everywhere, landing at her feet," she said, reaching up, touching the scar on her neck.

Ren turned back, glancing at his father. "When they returned to the house, she found several items in her hair and folds of the dress."

"Anything of interest?"

"Thirty pieces of gold and silver, along with the necklace and earrings you were wearing."

"Did she keep the treasure?"

"When father asked her to be his wife, she said they must first bury their pasts. The jewels, coins, locket, and ledgers were placed in a chest and given to Aunt Delphine. I believe it is buried on holy ground or at the bottom of the swamp."

Morlanna could hear their friends laughing behind her. "Sometimes burying the past and moving forward is for the best."

"We'll move forward together," he said, kissing her.

"Ren, Petit, we should leave. There is much for us to celebrate."

She smiled, patting Ren's arm. "You should tell them."

"Do you think they will be upset?"

"Only because they weren't there. I need a few minutes."

"When you are ready. Father, I have something to tell you," he said, walking away.

Morlanna could hear everyone cheering when Ren announced their marriage. She stepped forward, remembering the bishop's face. This experience forced her to realize a battle took place every day between good and evil, externally and internally. She took the time and changed the reflection in the mirror, proving the bishop wrong. Each day since being saved from the palace, she spent time helping the poor and orphans promising to make a difference no matter how small the gesture. Her faith had been renewed with prayers at mass alongside Ren. The people you love and care about, like the ones behind her, made the difference between light and dark.

About the Author

Janet began writing in 2009 while still a full-time travel nurse. She writes in multiple genres from Historical fiction to Paranormal thriller. Not to say she doesn't have a sense of humor. Her E-book You Just Can't leaves you smiling if not laughing.

In 2022, her flash fiction story *The Holiday Slayer* was a runner-up in the Women On Writing contest.

She has short stories in two different anthologies. Tales of Texas III and Nothing Ever Happens in Fox Hollow. A recent publication of a poem in Upon Arrival: Transitions, is something new for her. She has become active with Tellables/Chatables with three stories that can be heard on Alexa.

Janet can be found in Fifty Great Writers you should be Reading published by The Author Show, as a winner for 2017 and 2018.

An overall category Grand Prize Winner for Chatelaine in Chanticleer Book Awards added to the thirty-five awards for The Look for me Series. Twenty-six awards to date have been given to her Paranormal Mystery Thriller series.

She was a peace officer at one time, promoted to the rank of Sergeant, and worked in a multi-city unit investigating questionable deaths and homicides.

Retired now living in her home on Galveston Island she spends the day sitting on the deck, writing, drinking good wine, and listening to the breakers.

Additional Titles- BY JANET K. SHAWGO

Multi-Award-Winning Historical Series Look for Me, Wait for Me, Find Me Again

Multi-Award-Winning Mystery/Thriller Archidaus and Legacy of Lies

Multi-Award-Winning Novella-Its For the Best

Women on Writing Finalist for flash fiction, The Holiday Slayer

Ebook Comedy - You Just Can't

Short Stories

Tales of Texas Volume III

Let the Grapes Grow

The Yellow Rose

Tellables/ Chatables

Sweet Penny Valentines Box of Chocolates

Dark Bitter Joy Halloween Box of Chocolates

An Inconvenience

Nothing ever happens in Fox Hollow Anthologies

Book 1-Mirror, Mirror

Book 2- The Tree

Upon Arrival: Transitions Poetry
Mother and Me

You can connect with me on:
○ http://www.jkshawgo.com

Made in the USA
Columbia, SC
07 February 2025

52742315R00088